# Take a Break

## A. W. Lambert

**Credits**
Cover Artist: A.W. Lambert
Editor: Christie L. Kraemer

Printed in the United States of America

# Dedication

To Val, without who this would not have happened.

# Prologue

Over the years, like many authors, I have delved into short story writing. In the early days attempting to hone my skills with submissions to magazines and short story competitions, erroneously thinking it to be an easy option: two thousand words instead of two hundred thousand-- got to be easier, right?? And again, later, when struggling with full length fiction, as an aid to break the dreaded block.

For whatever reason, both before and now, between novels, I have always found short story writing relaxing and a great pleasure. And, yes, it has more than once helped me break through that difficult brain fade period and move on.

Within these pages you will find twenty-five short stories that, for a variety of reasons, I have written over the years. They average approximately 1700 words, each story taking around ten minutes of your time. There is absolutely no theme and they are in no particular sequence or categorised in any way. Indeed to read from cover to cover would probably be a mistake. Better to just drift back and forth, picking at random, which by the way, is exactly how they have been put together. You will find each different, each hopefully a pleasant little read. Some involve ghostly goings on, others a little detective work and still others are a tad goofy; just a little nonsense with something, hopefully, to raise a smile.

When taking that welcome break, cup of tea or coffee in hand, this is a little book which can literally be dipped into at any point for a ten minute relaxing read.

# 100 NOT OUT

It was Sunday morning and Detective Inspector Reginald Hardacre was feeling very sorry for himself. He firmly believed he had the flu. Not man-flu men were ridiculed for, but real flu. Had to be, because he hadn't felt so bad for a very long time and weren't they saying there was a lot of it about? Mrs Hardacre had shown very little sympathy.

"It's your own fault. At your age, if you really feel so bad, you should stay at home; stay in bed. It's the weekend, for goodness sake."

But she knew as well as he did he wouldn't. He never did. In good health or bad, the Force had been his life since his raw recruit days all those years before. Even now, with only a couple of years to retirement, it was just the same. Weekend or not, if something hit and the Superintendent called...

This time, a missing person and not just any missing person. The local Labour Party candidate had mysteriously disappeared while out on the campaign trail. How the hell could that happen? Hardacre remembered how pleased he had been that with the local elections in full swing he was no longer part of the uniform branch; all that patrolling, policing meetings and looking after individuals so full of their own self-importance. No thanks pal, he was finished with all of that.

Yeah, right.

3

"Top of the list, Reggie." The Super' had snapped down the telephone. He was probably making the call as he left for his Sunday round of golf. "We need to be on it. Like now"

*Like the 'we' bit? Thanks a lot mate.*

He'd managed to organise a large mug of hot, very strong and very sweet tea when he'd arrived at the station and with its help he had just swallowed two extra strength paracetamols. Cupping the still half full mug between his stubby fingers, he relaxed with a sigh back into the old chair. He stared into space, thinking, taking advantage of the few quiet moments before life erupted as he knew at any second it would.

And it did.

The familiar knock, when inevitably it came, was more a club hammer being applied to the other side of his office door than a knock. It was followed, with only the slightest of pauses, with the door being kicked open.

"Morning, guv', lovely morning." The vision, the greeting was always the same, rain or shine. The huge brutish looking young man standing in the doorway looked completely out of place, as he did every morning, holding the two dainty cups and saucers in his banana sized mitts.

"Oh, you've already got one," he boomed, stopping uncertainly and looking down at the mug clasped in his boss's hands.

Chester McCullock was without doubt the best Detective Constable Hardacre had ever had assigned to him. He was also the biggest, the loudest and the most overpowering. Feeling as he did today, Hardacre would have welcomed young Chester turning the volume down just a tad. He said nothing, though, just nodded to the chair opposite while at the same time holding out his free hand. Taking the offered cup he poured its contents into the mug he was still holding. "Could empty a bloody horse trough today," he rasped. "Right, what've you got for me?"

McCullock reached for his note book. "6.30pm yesterday afternoon. The Labour band wagon was on a roll canvassing the Barnsdale estate area. There was a whole bunch of 'em but they divided their forces, each being allotted a particular area. They agreed to meet sometime later at a pub." He looked across at Hardacre. "The Bull. You know it, guv?"

Hardacre nodded, his nose wrinkling. He knew the pub and guessed had the Labour candidate known it as well, he would have probably chosen another venue.

"Anyway they split up and the Labour candidate, name of Trench, went off down Marsden Street."

"And they haven't seen him since?"

"Her," McCullock said without looking up from his note book.

"What?"

"Her," the Constable repeated. "The Labour candidate is a her. Ms Julia Trench."

Hardacre sighed and took another swig at the tea.

Thirty minutes later Chester ground the car into the kerb and hauled on the hand brake. Hardacre eased himself out, wincing as, on the other side, the driver's door was slammed shut, the car rocking alarmingly at the impact. Chester, completely unaware of his superior's reproachful glare, stomped round the car, his mountainous six-foot-four frame towering over the other's short, stubby figure.

"Okay, guv'?"

Shaking his head, Hardacre turned and surveyed the area. Marsden Street, located almost in the centre of the Barnsdale estate, one of the more run down areas of the district.

"Okay, so take me through it one more time. And let's have some detail," he growled.

Again the young detective referred to his note book. "It seems Ms Trench and her helpers, there were four of them, arrived here at about six. They split the area into segments, each being allocated several streets to cover. They agreed to meet at seven thirty at The Bull. According to the others, Ms Trench headed off down there." He pointed toward the narrow, shabby looking street. "That was the last any of them saw of her."

"The rest of them met at The Bull as agreed?"

"Yes. It seems they waited for almost an hour; they said until about eight thirty. At first they weren't worried because Ms Trench was apparently notorious for taking her time over this sort of thing. She preached it regularly apparently, demanding they all donate as much time as was necessary to the voters."

"So, okay, they waited. Then what?"

"Then they began to get concerned and decided to go and see if they could find her. Again they split up and searched the streets. There was no sign of Ms Trench, but a couple of streets away they found this lying on top of a dust bin." He handed the Inspector a clip board.

"What's this?" The Inspector scanned the board and the sheets of paper attached to it.

"Apparently Ms Trench's idea," Chester grinned. "The others weren't so keen, but she insisted. They had to use it when canvassing." McCullock pointed to the sheets secured to the board. "The same proforma for everyone; used to make notes of the responses on the doorstep. They record who they talk to, their views, what they think are the important issues of the day. And of course, most important, who they say they're going to vote for. By collating all the returns they can get a rough idea how they stand in the polls."

Hardacre nodded. "Yeah, I would guess *rough* would be an apt description for this area too." He flicked through the wodge of proformas clipped to the board, studying each sheet for several moments. "So what are you telling me here?"

6

"Well y'see, they all have their own board, guv, and they assured me this one belongs to Ms Trench. It's the one she was using."

"They're sure about this?"

"Yup, they're certain. No doubt about it apparently. Y'see she always insisted on doing her own thing, taking her own notes, the lot."

Hardacre handed the clip board back to McCullock, turning and looking at the houses around them. It was obvious some of the tenants were still trying hard to maintain a semblance of respectability, others were completely run down, their tenants, probably unemployed, having long since given up the struggle. A few were not even occupied. "Our inner city wonderland," he sighed.

Despite it being a chilly, overcast day, Hardacre felt hot and clammy. A headache was beginning to form behind his eyes. "Bloody flu," he groaned as they turned back toward the car.

"So what's the next move, guv?" They were heading back to the station; McCullock at the wheel, Hardacre huddled miserably beside him.

"Uniform and a complete search of the area," the Inspector growled. "And you to the council offices. Get me an up-to-date listing of tenants on the estate, particularly Marsden Street. Drop me off and get to it right away."

"Er, its Sunday, guv."

Hardacre glowered sideways. "So?"

"The council offices; they won't be open."

"You're working, aren't you?"

"Well yeah, but..."

"No buts, Constable. Get the council clerk or whoever does the business down there out of bed or out of the pub, wherever he is. I want that list and I want it like yesterday, understand?"

"I'm on it." McCullock grinned, relishing the short, clipped instructions from his idol. He had come to recognise the signs. It meant the boss's brain had already clicked into gear, the cogs were turning. It was why he had applied for a position in the Criminal Investigation Department in the first place. Then to be put with Reggie Hardacre, one of the most experienced and revered officers in the force, he couldn't have asked for more. There were none better than his boss in full swing and McCullock thanked his lucky stars for that. He pushed his foot firmly on the throttle, unaware, as the car shot forward, of the apprehensive sidelong glance from his suffering boss.

~ * ~

The search of the Barnsdale estate had hardly begun when the officer in charge was given a message from Hardacre. He acted swiftly and the house in question was soon surrounded. The pounding on the front door had the desired effect and the two young men exiting the back door at speed were quickly apprehended. The petrified, but totally unharmed Ms Trench was found securely bound, gagged and dumped unceremoniously beneath a very grubby kitchen sink.

Later, back at his office, Hardacre sat cradling yet another large mug of steaming tea. More paracetamols had followed those before and though he was not prepared to admit it just yet, he had a distinct feeling he was beginning to feel better.

"So it wasn't planned then?"

Hardacre looked across at Chester's eager hulk sitting opposite, his whole demeanour hungry for explanation. "Nope. It was just coincidence."

The detective constable leaned forward, a deep frown creasing his forehead. "Coincidence?"

"Uh-Huh. The two young tearaways were using the house as a doss. When Ms Trench knocked on the door they were high on drugs and their stupefied brains came up with the idea of kidnap. It was a spur of the moment thing. They were potless and needed cash."

"But that's stupid. How on earth did they think they could get away with that?"

"Nothing is impossible when cocaine rules. You can even fly if you want to. Plenty have tried." Hardacre shook his head sadly. "Anyway, other than battering her pride a little, they didn't harm Ms Trench. In fact when the drugs began to wear off and they realised what they'd done, they were just as terrified as she was."

"But I still don't understand how you worked it out, guv. McCullock scratched the back of his head. "How did you know she would be in that house?"

Hardacre pushed the Labour candidate's clip board across the desk toward his young detective. "We were lucky to find this," he said. "But it wasn't until you got the list from the council it dawned on me." Pausing, he drank some of the now cooling tea. "You see, the council list indicated a number of the properties were unoccupied, right?"

McCullock nodded, but the deep frown remained.

"Look at the sheet, man," Hardacre growled, but with a broad grin. "They said she was a stickler for detail, didn't they? She made a note of all the houses she called at and whether the occupants were at home or not; whether they were in or out. Trouble was, with some houses unoccupied, there were more out than there were in. Ms Trench had recorded so many 'outs' that when she got to one where somebody actually answered the door she didn't record 'in' she wrote '100 not out'. Look at the last entry on her sheet; she even underlined it." He sat back contentedly and drained the mug.

McCullock scanned the sheet attached to the clipboard. "100 not out," he said thoughtfully then, a slow smile of realisation spreading, he reached for the council tenant's list, quickly turning the pages. He read out loud the appropriate entry: Number 100 Marsden Street--*Unoccupied*. Open mouthed he looked across at his boss. "Bloody brilliant."

"It has been said before," Detective Inspector Reginald Hardacre said smugly. Yes, now he was sure; he certainly was feeling very much better.

# THE BEST OF BOTH WORLDS

In his previous life he had been part of a motorcar. But not just any part of any motorcar. No, he'd come from the bonnet of a genuine Rolls Royce. Now there's a pedigree for you. Admittedly it had been a very old Rolls Royce; well, it wouldn't have been scrapped and recycled if it hadn't been, would it? But old or not, there weren't many metal toy soldiers that could say they had come from a genuine Rolls Royce, were there? And even now, in his new Grenadier Guard form, just like the old Rolls, he could boast he had been made in England. He was extremely proud of that, too.

He snuggled down comfortably in the darkness, the preformed polystyrene packing hugging his shape. There were ten of them, he thought, although it could be twelve. He couldn't be absolutely sure; the packing process was so quick it had been difficult to count. But they were all the same as him, all standing proud in their beautifully coloured, immaculate uniforms, all positioned in a neat row in the box. The journey from the factory had been quite uncomfortable; the vehicle carrying them bouncing around a great deal. Not like he was used to, he thought with a smile, remembering the smoothness of the old Rolls. In a Rolls Royce, even an old one, there was hardly a bump at all.

Anyway, all that was over now and they were safely packed on the shelf in the shop. He knew they were in the shop because he had heard the shop assistant being told what to do by the shop owner.

"Pack the boxes on the shelf," he'd said. "We'll open them in the morning, make a display."

A display. He couldn't wait. He remembered the Rolls Royce when it was new. Now that was what you could call a display. Standing magnificent in the show room. Polished every day, everybody wanting to touch the gleaming bodywork. He was bigger then, of course, a whole bonnet, and so proud. But it didn't really matter how big or how small you were, did it? Now he might be just a toy soldier, but he was nonetheless proud. After all he was a Grenadier Guard and some would say that was even better than being a Rolls Royce.

The night passed slowly with lots of whispering, everyone introducing themselves to their neighbours. And as good soldiers they counted themselves. He was right, there were ten. He was somewhere in the middle of the row, Harry on his right side and Bob on his left. In his previous life Harry had been a bicycle frame; he didn't know which type. And Bob couldn't be absolutely sure, but he thought he had originated from an old frying pan. He admitted he wasn't very proud of that, but it didn't matter now because, like the rest of them, he was a brand new, shiny Grenadier Guard. As for the others, none of them could boast anything like a Rolls Royce.

At last morning came. The box was lifted down from the shelf and the lid removed. As the light flooded in he stood straight as he could, thrusting out his chest and clutching his rifle rigidly to his shoulder, exactly as he was sure a Grenadier Guard would do.

It was a wonderful display and covered almost the entire shop window. Tanks and trucks, their pennants flying proudly, stood in rows at the rear. Staff cars with officers sitting stiffly in the back seats manoeuvred themselves in and out of the other vehicles. Dispatch riders, some with sidecars, sat astride their motorcycles ready for action and cavalrymen mounted on strutting horses formed orderly rows to one side. And in the front, at the centre of the whole display, the infantrymen of the Grenadier Guards. It was a magnificent sight.

When he'd been pulled from the box, the shop assistant had viewed him with an enthusiastic eye.

"Best we've had yet, don't you think?" The words were like music to his ears and he desperately wanted to shout out he had once been a Rolls Royce. He couldn't, of course. Instead he gloried in the feeling that after being the very best of one thing, he was now the best of another.

Other boxes had been emptied and the soldiers stood in neat rows facing forward, looking proudly out through the shop window, nearest of all to the admiring glances of the people passing in the street. And to his utter delight he had found himself positioned on the very end of the very front row, only inches from the window. He could feel the power of the whole display behind him. He could hear the roar of the tanks and the trucks, the sharp rattle of the motorcycle exhausts and the impatient stamping of the horse's hooves. He could hear the officers shouting their commands and the whole army preparing itself for battle.

The shop owner had left the shop, wandering out onto the pavement, studying the display; his handiwork. He stood for some time, fingering his chin, a frown on his face. Then nodding to himself he returned to the shop.

"Something wrong?" the shop assistant asked.

The owner nodded. "Something missing."

"Missing?" repeated the assistant.

"Yes. It's those Grenadiers."

He felt his tiny heart sink. What could be wrong? Hadn't the assistant said they were the best yet? Hadn't he said that? He glanced to one side, down the row. It was perfectly straight. The soldiers, every one immaculate; their newly painted uniforms gleaming. So what could be wrong?

"It's the one on the end," he heard the shop owner say. "Take him out, he's not right."

The one on the end? But that was him. How could he not be right? How could he, with his pedigree, be wrong? There had to be a mistake.

But there was no mistake and utter devastation enveloped him as he felt himself being lifted from his place of honour in the front of the magnificent display.

They took him to the back of the shop where they laid him on a workbench in the corner. The shop owner opened a drawer and for what seemed forever searched among its contents.

"Ah," he said, finally making his way back to the bench.

It took just a few moments and when it was over the shop owner studied his finished work with some satisfaction. "That's much better", he said, polishing the little figure carefully with a soft cloth, reminding him again of the car show room all those years before.

They placed him back in position, but this time not exactly the same position as before. This time he was placed in the front and to one side, looking across at the row of other soldiers. The shop owner again wandered out onto the pavement, this time a wide smile spreading across his face. Nodding happily, he made his way back into the shop.

"Much better," he said to the assistant. "How can you have a whole battalion of Grenadier Guards without a Sergeant?"

The little soldier looked down at the brand new gleaming chevrons on the arms of his jacket and pulled himself up even taller than before. He felt an immense pride as he looked down the row of *his* men. He knew it was a great honour to be promoted to a sergeant in the Grenadier Guards, but it was only fitting, wasn't it? After all he had been a Rolls Royce, and you can't get much better than that, can you?

14

# COUNTRY LIFE

The train gave a jolt and began to slow. He glanced up from the newspaper, the familiar sinking feeling creeping into his stomach. Not today, of all days, not today. It was his daughter's birthday, for goodness sake. He rubbed at the condensation-covered window, peering out into the chilled November darkness, trying to see where they were, but unable to do so. Maybe they had just eased down, he thought hopefully, a slower part of the track. But the deceleration continued until the train was barely crawling and the usual anger began to well inside him.

He hated the railways, loathed them. They were the very worst way to travel; noisy and jarringly uncomfortable, always crowded with no chance at all of peace or privacy. They were never on time and worst of all, when you needed them most, they let you down completely. And what galled him more than anything? There was no alternative. To drive the car into town every day would be impossible. The railway was the only option. Fuming as he had so many times over recent years, he felt the train judder to a halt, the familiar, helpless silence surrounding him.

If only Jill would listen to him. Hadn't they seen it many times on TV? Get out of the rat race; sell the house and buy a place in the country, a better quality of life. Only the previous evening he had again tried to reason with her.

15

"But you are a town person and you love your work," she had argued. "What would you do in the country? How would we live? And the children, what about their schooling?"

"I could learn to be a country person, couldn't I? There must be something I could do." It sounded lame, but he was sure he could find some way of earning a living. "And they do have schools in the country, you know."

"But what's wrong with this place? Nice house, in the suburbs. I mean, the journey is only twenty minutes."

"Yeah, twenty minutes when things go right," he humphed, "which is almost never. It drives me mad."

"But you have a wonderful home and a job you love. Life is never perfect, you can't have everything."

As it had so many times before, the conversation had faded to silence, their eyes drifting back to the television.

Unusually he was alone in the carriage. He had stayed later than he normally would have, engrossed in his work, forgetting the time and thankful, when he checked, there was a later train. Even so he had only just managed it, sprinting along the platform, boarding only seconds before the train left the station. Normally, on the earlier train, seats were at a premium and he was surprised and delighted to find the carriage empty. A comfortable, peaceful journey, he had thought.

The remote, metallic sound of the driver's voice broke the silence. Due to technical problems there would be a delay and it was difficult to say how long. The good news was they had managed to pull into a small station, not usually a stopping point, and passengers were welcome to alight and stretch their legs. Every effort would be made to ensure the delay was as short as possible.

He slumped back in the seat, the familiar tightness in his chest. "Damn, damn, damn." They would be waiting at home; the cake, the candles, the expectant, excited smiles as he came through the door, knowing something special would be in daddy's briefcase. Damn the bloody railways. He pushed himself out of the seat and angrily dragged on his coat.

Out on the platform he squinted up at the station sign, frowning; he thought he knew the name of all the stations on his route, but the name on the board was unfamiliar. He shook his head; strange that. He shrugged; no point in trying to unravel the mysteries of the railways. He dug into his pocket and pulled out the mobile.

"Ain't no use you trying that there 'ere."

"What?" He glanced up, startled by the voice; the short, rotund individual appearing from the tiny waiting room door.

"Them there mobile things. Ain't no use 'ere, you know."

"You mean there's no signal here?"

"Don't know nothin' 'bout signals," he said, smiling benevolently. "Just know they don't work 'ere."

Dejectedly he pushed the phone back into his pocket. "You work on the station?" he asked.

The man nodded. "Man and boy, nearly forty years."

"Is there a telephone I could use? It's my daughter's birthday, you see, I need to phone."

Lips pursed, the man thought for some moments then shook his head. "No phone 'ere," he said finally. "Nothing stops 'ere, y'see. Not normally, that is."

He could feel the tension building in him. "Is there one anywhere then, somewhere close? I'm willing to pay, of course."

Again there was a long pause. "Might be one at the 'orse."

"The horse?"

"'Sright, the 'orse and groom."

Hopes rose. "The Horse and Groom. Is it far?"

The man took him by the sleeve and led him to the end of the platform, peering round the end of the station building and pointing. "See the light?"

He followed the direction of the man's finger; a light glittered dimly at the end of a lane he guessed to be a couple of hundred metres long.

He didn't know how long the delay would be, but he would have to risk it. He borrowed a torch from the station employee.

The torch began to falter after just a few minutes and he soon realised he would have to use it sparingly, switching it on only every few metres to check ahead. But the torch soon gave up and all he could do was keep his eye on the light ahead and press on. Unseen bushes, some with spiteful thorns, pulled at his suit and his shoes sunk into slushy hollows. At one point he stumbled, dropping to his knees among the hedgerow, his hands groping among painful stinging nettles. Reaching out, he groped for support, finding a rough post, clutching at it gratefully with both hands and pulling himself to his feet.

Finally, with some relief, he pushed his way through the door of the Horse and Groom. The bar was dimly lit and the flames from a fire burning in a wide grate reflected on the shadowed walls. He felt his throat tighten as he breathed the warm air uncomfortably thick with fumes from the burning logs. The only other customers, two men sitting at a table in the corner, stopped talking as he entered.

The landlord, leaning casually against the bar, turned toward him, his eyes scanning from head to toe before speaking. "Come up the lane, then?" he said finally, a hint of a smile touching the corners of his mouth.

He looked down at his mud-encrusted shoes, his stained trousers, a jagged tear in the pocket of his jacket. Dammit, he had only bought the suit the week before. He did his best to return the smile. "Yes, the train, it's broken down. I was wondering if I could use your telephone. My daughter, it's her birthday, you see." He approached the bar, conscious of the stinging rash growing on the backs of his hands.

"Train? Broke down?"

He nodded. "Yes. They managed to pull into the station."

The landlord shook his head. "Trains don't stop 'ere. Ain't done that for years."

"No, so I understand, but this time they..."

"Daughter's birthday, you say?" The landlord broke in, dismissing the subject.

"Oh, yes."

"How old would she be then?"

"Er, how old?" He hesitated, surprised at the question, at the same time realising from a sudden unpleasant smell beginning to permeate the warmth of the bar the mud on his boots and trousers was probably not mud after all. "She's ten."

The landlord's smile widened. "Ten." He looked toward the other two men. "Hear that lads" he said. "His daughter's ten today."

Both men smiled lifting their hands in salute. "Lovely age is ten," one of them said.

He smiled dutifully at the two men and turned back to the landlord. "The phone, do you think...?"

The landlord was concentrating on pulling a pint. "'Ere," he said, putting the frothing glass on the bar. "Have one on the house." He chuckled. "Ten. That's nice."

"Er, thank you, that's very kind, but the telephone, I wonder if..." He reached for the glass, suddenly realising that his mouth was dry.

"Well now that looks nasty." The landlord leaned across the bar, taking hold of his hand before it could reach the glass.

He looked down at his hand, noticing for the first time the nasty graze across his knuckles. "Oh, it's nothing, just a graze."

"Just a graze?" The landlord again looked toward the men at the table. "Just a graze," he repeated. "'Ear that lads? Just a graze, 'e says. That's what old 'Arry Spriggs said, remember?"

The men nodded solemnly in unison. "That's what he said, alright."

19

"Harry Spriggs?"

The landlord bowed his head. "Miss old 'Arry, we do. Ain't no such thing as just a graze out 'ere, lad." He held onto the hand. "Never know what might be in that right now. Just like old 'Arry. Best let the missus see to that 'fore much longer," he insisted.

"Thank you, that is kind of you, but I should get back to the train and I would appreciate it if I could use the telephone."

"Ah yes, now 'bout that telephone. It was the storm, you see. Day 'fore yesterday it was. Probably a day or two before they get to us. Out in the sticks as we are. No priority y'see."

~ * ~

He woke to the sun streaming through the window, the sweet smell of freshly laundered sheets mingling with Jill's perfume as she breathed gently beside him. He rolled onto his back and let his eyes wander around the bedroom; recently decorated with the new bedroom furniture, everything clean and fresh.

His mind drifted back to the previous evening, recalling his dismay when told the telephone lines were down and his intense annoyance at the landlord's resigned acceptance of the situation. He hadn't touched the beer, hurriedly leaving the Horse and Groom, terrified the train would leave before he had time to re-negotiate his way back along the dreaded lane. And it almost had, jolting into motion at the same time as he had staggered back onto the platform. Wrenching open the nearest carriage door, he had stumbled inside. And this time the compartment was not empty. The remainder of the journey was punctuated by wrinkled noses, sniffs and uncomfortable little coughs as the other passengers stole surreptitious glances toward him.

He had arrived home late but thankfully not too late. There had been little time to explain his condition. The evil smelling clothes were hurriedly encased in a plastic bag and tossed disgustedly into a bin. His heavily contaminated shoes left on the back step. A hurried but no less wonderful bath had followed with soothing cream on his burning hands and a fresh plaster on that graze. Then finally the clean clothes and the fun of his daughter's party.

He felt her move beside him and turning, realised she was watching him.

"Penny for them," she said.

"I was just thinking maybe the journey to work isn't so bad after all," he said. "It's a slow process and sometimes gets to me, I have to admit, but maybe you're right. Maybe we should stay as we are."

She rolled over and faced him. "What brought this on?"

"Oh, nothing really. It's just that, well maybe country life isn't all it's cracked up to be. Know what I mean?"

# ANCESTORS

You would have thought having been around as long as I have nothing much would shock me. Well, until a short time ago, I would have thought the same, but…

I remember it well, how could I not? Relaxing in my favourite chair, I was quietly reading when the door burst open and in they roared. Crashing and banging, screaming and wailing, I've never experienced anything like it in my life. I'm sure I must have leapt a foot in the air. I left the book where it had fallen and fled the room, listening terrified from the other side of the door. Fortunately, they didn't follow me. In fact, so busy were they with their rushing around and caterwauling, it was as if they hadn't noticed me at all.

For some time I tried to identify the noises, the weird sounds, without success. Then, finally plucking up courage, I eased the door open just a crack. There were several of them and they were frighteningly grotesque, drifting aimlessly about the room, pushing and shoving and communicating in unintelligible grunts and cackles. I'd seen nothing quite like them before and have to admit to being terrified. I quietly closed the door and retreated to the other end of the house to think.

This sort of thing wasn't entirely new to me, of course. After all, a stately home, its history going back generations, is subject to such manifestations. Many of my ancestors, all Dukes and Earls of the realm, have returned, wandering the corridors, bemoaning some wrongdoing or other, or just maintaining their right of occupation. Indeed, in some cases, the disruption is such that the assistance of the clergy has been required to ease the troubled forebear to his final resting place on the other side.

Algernon was a typical example. The third Duke on my father's side. Algernon was poisoned by his eldest son Cedric, who being up to his neck in debt as a result of an over indulgence in life's pleasures, was desperate for the title and the riches that went with it. To protect the family name, the record shows Algernon's demise as being of natural causes, but for some years Algernon made regular visits wailing of his right to the truth. Exorcism was not required in Algernon's case, however, because his visits came to a natural halt when Cedric also met his end in some particularly gruesome manner. I suspect, seeing justice as finally being done, Algernon was content to R.I.P. Unlike Cuthbert who, if I remember rightly, was Algernon's great, great, great grandfather and still makes the occasional appearance to this day.

Cuthbert was the fifth Earl and once ninth in line to the throne. He was affectionately known as Cuthbert the Clod, though not to his face, of course. In death Cuthbert is exactly the same as he was in life: in a word, and you must forgive me speaking of a titled ancestor in such a way, stupid. Cuthbert's offspring had no aspirations toward the title or the wealth that went with it. Even if they had, there would have been little need to go to the extremes of Algernon's eldest. They had only to be patient. For it was clear to anyone with half a brain, Cuthbert would require no help whatsoever in eventually shuffling himself off this mortal coil.

You see Cuthbert was convinced he could fly and, as was expected, eventually proved he really could. The problem was he only managed it for approximately three seconds; the time taken for him to travel unassisted from the main turret to the freshly planted rockery just

23

outside the great hall. The head gardener was not amused and who could blame him?

As I said, in death as in life. Even now, on a still moonlit night, Cuthbert can be seen floating happily down from that very same turret. He gives me a wave from time to time and I have to say, his landings have greatly improved.

Forgive me for drifting into the lives and deaths of my ancestors, but the point I'm trying to make is, unlike the current intrusion, neither Algernon nor Cuthbert had a disruptive influence. Even if Algernon had continued his quest for truth, exorcism would have been unnecessary. After all what harm could a sad old man wandering the corridors bemoaning his lot do? And as for Cuthbert: a happy three-second appearance on the occasional moonlit night? It would be cruel to spoil his fun, wouldn't it?

This latest incursion is different however. Extensive disruption is already taking place, and as far as I can see it can only get worse. This, I have to say with deep regret, is much more like Adulphus the Angry.

Here I must beg your forgiveness. Just saying the name is speaking the unspeakable and leaves a foul taste in one's mouth. You see for many generations the name Adulphus has remained unspoken, and those who have studied the family tree could be forgiven for asking where he sat in line. I bring him into the picture reluctantly and only to make my point.

Adulphus was the first Germanium blood injected into the family. He was angry from birth; some say because he slithered into the world at such speed that, before an elderly and extremely slow midwife could stop his bullet like breakout, his head encountered one of the four bedposts. It was said, in later years, when as a result of the copious amounts of alcohol consumed, the wig he habitually wore slid precariously to one side, the deep groove in his skull could still be seen. That may or may not be so, but one thing is sure, the anger remained with him throughout his life.

24

As well as being angry, Adulphus was ruthlessly arrogant and obsessed with his own immortality. He was desperate to be remembered in the history books and he didn't care how he did it. His many deeds were legendary, each as despicable as the last and each requiring the most gigantic efforts by those around him to prevent the family name from being thrown into disrepute. His last and most egotistical act, and the one that brought his final downfall, though not officially recorded, is still here to be seen.

Adulphus felt the need to be immortalized in oils. More, he wanted to be depicted as a saint. Yes, I know, others have followed the same path, but Adulphus? Anyway, a most famous artist of the time, though familiar with the Adulphus reputation and terrified of damaging his own reputation, was eventually and very reluctantly enticed by the promise of a huge payout to accept the commission. And the result was a triumph; an enormous canvas with Adulphus depicted saintly centre stage surrounded by the purest of semi clad nymphs and angels.

Now a leopard never changes its spots, and true to character, though secretly delighted, Adulphus feigned disappointment. Though hanging onto the portrait-he was no fool-he refused to pay the artist one penny. The artist, like all artists, was stony broke and furious, and having spent all that time on the canvas, he was going to remain that way. He vowed revenge and a little later gained entry to the house at the dead of night. The following morning when Adulphus pranced into the great hall to admire his masterpiece, which, by the way, was already taking pride of place over the great fireplace, he was met with the most grotesque of images. His regal looking head had been replaced by that of a grinning donkey and the nymphs and angels replaced by prancing, wicked faced elves and pixies. The donkey wore a wig which had slipped to one side revealing a deep groove in its skull along which lay a steaming sausage.

Enraged, Adulphus felt, as he had often done in the past, an overpowering need to beat someone. Also, as in the past, the nearest victim was his long-suffering wife, Esmeralda, who had yet to rise from her slumbers. Adulphus roared up the stairs and burst into the main bedroom where in his rage he failed to notice Esmeralda's pet poodle curled up on the floor snoozing peacefully. Stepping squarely on the unfortunate animal he was catapulted headlong toward the bed.

It is said Adulphus exited this world against the very same bedpost he had met on entry. His wife, it is recorded, was very distraught: she thought she was entitled to at least another hour before having to rise. So you see, such a despicable individual was Adulphus that, far from being immortalized, all mention of his existence was expunged from the family records.

You may ask why I have taken the trouble to even mention Adulphus. Well I do so because, unlike Algernon and Cuthbert, Adulphus did need to be exorcised. Indeed only the efforts of the highest level of the cloth--Adulphus insisted nothing lower than a Bishop would suffice-- was able to bring an end to his constant moaning and wailing and only with the promise the offending painting be removed forever.

So with such experience behind me, why am I not evicting these latest apparitions? Why am I not, at this very moment, heading for the Bishop's palace? Well, having studied them closely, I now know these extraordinary creatures with their metal pierced bodies and their unintelligible language, with the strange shaped implements hanging around their necks and the dreadful wailing and screeching coming from the huge black boxes stacked high in the great hall, are a completely new phenomena. These evil looking devils are not wayward, lost spirits of my ancestors. In fact, though wayward they maybe, spirits they are definitely not and even the Bishop himself would be powerless against them.

I have listened long and intently and though the greater part of their strange language is still beyond me, I have been able to interpret just a few phrases. It appears these creatures are known as *Pop Stars* and from their babblings I understand them to be very rich. I also believe, to my utter dismay, they now own my ancestral home.

26

With this knowledge I have retired in despair to the attic where few ever venture. I still have my books to pass the time and I will of course make the occasional foray downstairs; my contract as the current house specter has several generations still to run and demands it. I will however, as I am far more terrified of my new tenants than they could ever be of me, keep my visits to a minimum--the occasional manifestation with the odd passing through a wall will suffice.

I doubt I will be lonely. Cuthbert, as he does from time to time, will pop in for his usual chats and if I need cheering up there is always Adulphus' portrait secretly tucked away in the corner. A generation or two will soon pass and with any luck things will return to normal.

# WORDS, JUST WORDS

The Superintendent glared across the desk. "Words, Inspector, you're just giving me words. Every newspaper is having a field day, the Chief Constable is chewing at my backside and all you can give me is words." He twirled his favourite, gold plated fountain pen between agitated fingers. "I need actions, Inspector, not words. This individual, whoever he is, must be caught and put away, and quick, d'you understand?"

Inspector Theodore Hardacre made his way back to his office, a wan smile touching his tired features. He had been in this position many times before. Never mind the circumstances: the extreme difficulties surrounding the case, the usual heavy workload, the shortage of manpower. None of this mattered. Just solve the case, catch the villain, and make us look good. He sometimes wondered if looking good was all that did matter these days.

He pushed through the door into his office, crossing to his desk and slumping dejectedly into his old battered chair. He was just twelve months away from retirement and as far as he was concerned, it couldn't come soon enough. There was a time when he would never have felt like this, however difficult a case. He was a street copper, always had been. He'd clawed his way up through the ranks, loving every minute of every chase, whether the outcome was good or bad, successful or otherwise. And though he said it himself, he'd had many more successes than failures. Now, however, things were different. There was too much red tape, too many politics. Also, though he hated to admit it, his own energy level had taken a serious dip over the last couple of years.

"Anything I can do, sir?"

Hardacre lifted weary eyes and surveyed detective constable Mark Chambers, his latest assistant, sitting at the small desk in the far corner of the office. Fresh faced with clear, intelligent, eyes, Chambers, eager to please, leaned toward his boss. Hardacre remembered the young man's impressive curriculum vitae: high grades at 'A' level, a degree in English and among the top five at Police College. A high-flyer and potential brass of the future. It was the way of the modern Police Force; the top brass getting younger and younger, high academics taking the place of years of graft and experience. Hell, Hardacre's own Chief Superintendent was just thirty-nine years old.

But even high flyers had to start somewhere, and Chambers, for a time anyway, was under the wing of Theodore Hardacre whose career spanned from a secondary modern education to a police constable pounding the streets and grafting progressively on to the heady heights of Police Inspector in the Criminal Investigation Department.

Hardacre sighed. "Yes, there is something you can do, Chambers. You can solve the Professor case for me. But before you do that, you can get us both a mug of tea from the canteen."

An early visit to the Super's office, particularly under this morning's circumstances, never started the day well. Tea, hot and strong with three sugars, was a must. Hardacre remembered with regret when a single cup without sugar would suffice. Still, he'd stopped smoking; that was something. The sugar? Well, at his age he needed the extra energy, didn't he?

He leaned back in his chair, the mug cradled to his chest. "So, let's go through it one more time."

Puffing his cheeks, Chambers studied the notes in front of him. "We have six burglaries over the last six months, one a month almost to the day. All large houses in their own grounds, moneyed families, cash and jewellery kept in the house. All entries were carried out at night and always when the owners were away. Only small stuff taken; cash, jewels, a few paintings, but only valuable miniatures, only things that could be carried in an average size holdall."

"And locations?"

"The suburbs. Draw a three mile circle around the city; they're all there."

Hardacre leaned forward. "And then there's the notes."

Chambers nodded. "One left at every house. Addressed to the police, taunting, challenging us to catch him if we can."

Hardacre sighed despondently, recalling his earlier meeting with the Superintendent. "And a copy sent to the local rag."

Chambers nodded. "Every time."

"And no finger prints, of course?"

"No sir. Plenty of smudges. At a guess I'd say rubber gloves."

"Clever sod," Hardacre mused.

"Yes sir. And well read, I think."

"Why do you say that?"

"It's the way the notes are written, sir. The words used. I don't think any ordinary, small time criminal would have that level of vocabulary."

"You consider all criminals uneducated then?"

Chambers shifted uncomfortably in his chair. "No sir, not at all. It's just some of the words used...well, I just don't see them coming from the mouth of your average man on the street, let alone a villain. And don't forget, he does sign himself The Professor."

Hardacre, frowning thoughtfully, nodded. "Yes, he does, doesn't he? Okay, so remind me of these words again."

Chambers flicked through the paperwork in front of him, grateful to be given the opportunity to explain. He pointed to one of the notes. "Here, when he's crowing about us never catching him. He uses the word 'unequivocal'".

Hardacre shrugged. "Nothing special about that, is there?"

"Maybe not, sir, but most people would use 'definite' wouldn't they?"

Hardacre thought for a beat. "Maybe. Does it mean the same thing?"

"No, not exactly, but most of us wouldn't know that and would use it anyway."

"I suppose." Hardacre sounded unconvinced.

"Okay, how about this then," Chambers went on quickly. "Here, he's describing his thoughts when filling his bag. He uses the word 'lucubrate'".

"What?"

"Lucubrate."

"Never heard of it."

"Exactly. It means to express your thoughts, particularly at night. Maybe someone working by candle light or a night light." He looked across at Hardacre, a grin spreading across his face. "Even I had to look that one up, sir. And here again," he selected another note, "when describing the police, he uses the word 'impuissant'".

"Impu what?"

"Impuissant. It means powerless or weak." He inclined his head questioningly. "Surely your average burglar wouldn't use words like that, would he?" He laughed. "Well not unless he'd swallowed a dictionary, anyway."

Hardacre leaned back in his chair, eyebrows puckered thoughtfully. "Unless he had swallowed a dictionary," he said quietly to himself. He sipped at the cooling tea, his mind dredging back. It was a very long time ago, but... A smile slowly spread across his face. "Surely not," he murmured.

"Sir?"

Hardacre dropped the mug onto his desk and pushed himself up out of his chair. "Chambers, it's the central library for us, and you're driving. Oh, and bring those notes with you."

At the library Hardacre pulled the book from the shelf. The Concise Oxford English Dictionary, he read from its cover. "Now that word again. Impu...what was it?"

Chambers pronounced the word slowly and spelled it out. Hardacre flicked quickly through the pages, his finger finally tracing its way down to the word.

"Bingo." A broad grin spread across his face.

~ * ~

The surveillance team had been in place for just four days when the arrest was made and the suspect brought in. Hardacre, sporting a satisfied smirk, led Chambers into the interview room. The atmosphere was close; thick with stale body odour and the faint, struggling efforts of disinfectant. As they entered, the small, balding man lounging at the table stood, smiled broadly and offered Hardacre his hand.

"Well, well Mr Hardacre," he said. "It has been a long time."

Hardacre shook the man's hand. "Ronnie 'The Wordsmith' Mitchell, as I live and breathe. I thought you'd taken the straight and narrow years back."

"So I did, Mr Hardacre. So I did. I cannot imagine why I've been escorted here today. After all, one should be able to have a quiet read in one's public library without being harassed by the local constabulary." The words dripped sincerity, but the smile stayed in place.

Hardacre turned to Chambers. "Let me introduce Mr Ronnie Mitchell, alias The Wordsmith, and now, I suspect, the Professor," he said. "Habitual burglar who has spent as much time in the local nick as he has tucked up at home with his long-suffering wife, Florrie. Ronnie got his nickname because back in the good old days, when inside, he was the regular scribe for those who wanted to write home, but didn't have the necessary skills to do so."

Mitchell nodded in agreement. "One should always be happy to help those less fortunate than one's self, Mr Hardacre."

"Ronnie is also an avid reader," Hardacre continued. "But he doesn't read any old thing. Oh no, Ronnie's favourite book, in fact Ronnie's only book, is the dictionary. Indeed it has been said as a child Ronnie swallowed a dictionary. Isn't that so Ronnie?"

The little man nodded with mock solemnity. "'Tis true, Mr. Hardacre. I can only admit to it." He looked up at Chambers. "You see I believe one's vocabulary is one's greatest asset, wouldn't you say so?"

Hardacre laughed. "That and the ability to break into other people's houses, of course."

Mitchell looked hurt. "How could you suggest such a thing, Mr Hardacre? I may have strayed once or twice in the past, but that is all behind me now. A misguided youth, you might say."

"Yes, the longest youth in history," Hardacre chortled.

The little man's eyes moved shiftily around the room, particularly noting the two interview tape recorders, their doors hanging open, the tapes disengaged. "I am intrigued to know however how you came to connect me with whatever crime you are at present investigating." He paused before continuing. "Not that I admit to any involvement, of course."

Hardacre smiled happily, knowing with certainty his next visit to the Superintendent's office would be far more amicable than the last. "It was the notes, Ronnie. A nice touch, but a step too far I think. You see DC Chambers thought villains wouldn't have the education to write such notes, and generally he was right. But then he mentioned someone must have swallowed a dictionary. Now who do you think that brought to mind, Ronnie?"

Mitchell frowned, puzzled. "But a note is a note, Mr Hardacre. Anyone could write a note. I mean it's only words, isn't it?"

"True," Hardacre agreed. "But when those very same words are found to be underlined in one's favourite book, the very same book one was later observed studying, pencil in hand, at the central library, then I'm afraid we must assume to have one..." A mock frown corrugating his forehead, Hardacre turned to Chambers. "Now I'm afraid I'm showing my lack of education, Chambers. What are the words I'm looking for?"

Chambers thought for only a second. "Bang to rights, sir?"

Hardacre smiled. "Only words, Chambers, only words." He sighed contentedly. "But so apt."

# WAITING FOR CHALKY

Do you believe in ghosts? No? Well, I don't blame you. No rational minded person would, would they? And as a lifelong soldier, there was no one more rational than me.

Thirty years; boy soldier to Lieutenant Colonel. Northern Ireland, The Falklands, Iraq, I'd seen them all; life and death in the raw you might say. No room for wishy-washy thoughts of a life thereafter where I came from. No, it was enjoy life while you can because when your times up, it's up, isn't it? It's over. Finished, right?

Yeah, well…maybe.

When I retired, my wife and I chose carefully. We had seen the rough side of life, now was the time for peace and quiet. And the public house in the little Norfolk village was just what we were looking for. It was in the perfect rural location and its projected takings, though nothing to write home about, when augmented by my military pension, would give us the comfortable retirement we had planned for so long.

My wife immediately joined the WI, helped out at the church and generally integrated into the local scene. I concentrated on running the pub and enjoying my retirement to the full; my evenings filled with the local characters and their stories, my spare time spent walking Buster the dog and exploring my new surroundings.

It was mid-September, the thirteenth to be exact. I remember it well because it was my birthday and six months to the day since we'd taken over the pub. The evenings were beginning to draw in and there was a hint of a change in the air, a lessening of the sun's strength. But it was still warm and I'd been walking since closing the pub after the lunchtime session. So engrossed was I in my exploring, I walked much further, stayed out longer, than I had intended. Feeling a little weary, I settled to rest on a grassy bank, my back against a large oak. I relaxed in the warm afternoon sunshine as Buster, head down, foraged relentlessly among the undergrowth, darting from one spot to the other, investigating every sound, every smell.

I have often asked myself since; did I doze, even rest my eyes for just a second? If I did I was unaware of doing so and yet suddenly he was there, standing over me, looking down, and smiling a sad, tired smile. He was young, no more than twenty or so and pale with soft, fair hair drifting over one eye. He wore a waist length, jerkin style, leather jacket and a scarf wound untidily around his neck. His trousers, a thick, dark worsted material, were tucked into heavy fur-lined boots. But what took my eye most of all was the nasty gash that ran from the hairline above his right temple to his chin. It was no longer bleeding, the blood thickly congealed and crusted, but I'd seen many wounds in my long military career and knew instantly this young man needed medical attention and quick.

I scrambled to my feet, my mind racing; the jerkin, the heavy boots, it had to be a motorcycle accident. I instinctively reached toward him, offering support, but he moved back a pace, out of reach. I stood, arms still extended, uncertain. "Are you okay?"

He nodded, the sad smile persisting. I noticed his eyes, focused on a point just above my head. I had seen the signs before. Concussion.

"Yes, we're all okay," he said, his words soft and dreamlike. "It's Chalky. We're just waiting for Chalky."

"Chalky? Was he with you? Is he hurt too?"

His head turned, his eyes now scanning the woodland behind me. "No, Chalky got out before. There was only time for him. But we can't leave him. We have to wait." He frowned, his eyes narrowing as if he had seen something in the undergrowth. He gave a half wave of his hand and shuffled uncertainly toward the trees.

"Wait," I called after him. "You need to see a doctor." I pulled out my mobile and held it up for him to see. "I can make a call, get an ambulance."

He hesitated, looking back, shaking his head. "Don't worry, old sport," he said. "Just waiting for Chalky, that's all." He turned and in seconds was lost among the trees. Common sense urged me to go after him, bring him back and call for help, but an inner something held me back and I just stood staring stupidly at the spot where he had disappeared.

Feeling pressure against my leg, I glance down. For some reason Buster cowered at my feet, his ears flattened to his head.

That evening, behind the bar, the vision of the young man haunted my thoughts. Earlier, immediately after returning from my walk, I'd telephoned the local police and reported the accident. Remembering the young man's words, "We're *all* okay", I reported, although I had only seen one person, there were probably more involved in the accident.

"Oi, what's this then?" I was snapped back to the present by the sharp retort. Old Len Bartlett, the pub's oldest and most faithful regular, stood before me, his pint pot extended. "I asked for mild. You know I always have mild. This isn't mild, it's bitter."

I took the pot from him. "Sorry, Len," I apologized. "Things on my mind," I emptied the pot, refilled it with his favourite and handed it back.

Len supped at the fresh liquid and smacked his lips, satisfied. "That's more like it. So what's the problem then?"

I related the story of my encounter with the young man. Slowly, as the tale unfolded, a smile spread across the old man's face. "And you reported it to the police?" he said when I had finished.

I nodded. "Strange though, they said they'd had no reports of any accidents in the area."

Len pursed his lips. "'Sright, 'cause there weren't none."

"Sorry?"

"You're privileged, lad," he said with conspiratorial wink. "Us that know, us old'ns don't talk about it, but looks like today you met one of the Romeo Victor crew."

"The what?"

"The Romeo Victor crew."

I studied the old boy across the bar. "What the hell are you talking about, Len?"

He took another long draught from the pot before answering. "I think it's time for you to meet our Arthur," he said finally.

The following day, after the lunchtime session, I closed the pub and followed Len to a tiny cottage on the outskirts of the village. A woman who I guess was in her late fifties answered our knock. She ushered us through to a tiny sitting room at the back of the cottage.

"Dad," she said, as we entered, "You've got visitors."

The old man was sitting in a high backed, winged armchair facing the window looking directly down the garden and out across open fields beyond. Despite his obvious age, he had a full head of pure white hair, a broad smile and eyes that sparkled mischievously.

Len dropped into a chair opposite the old man. He grinned up at me. "I'd like you to meet our Arthur," he said. "Arthur White." He turned back to the old man. "Arthur, this is our new publican," he said. "Yesterday he was out walking and guess what?"

38

The old man turned his twinkling eyes toward me. He chuckled happily. "Met the boys, did you?"

"Sorry?" Confused I turned to Len for an explanation.

"Just the one, Arthur" Len said, his eyes still on the old man. "The blonde lad."

"Ah, that'll be the Skipper. Must be getting impatient."

"I'm not surprised," Len laughed. "They've waited long enough."

Totally mystified, I looked from one old man to the other.

Old Arthur pointed to a hard backed chair, motioning me to sit alongside him, waiting for me to settle before raising a bony finger and pointed to a spot in the sky above the distant field.

"We'd made it to about there," he said. "Pretty shot up, we were; only the two engines at full power. But old Romeo Victor was a wonderful Kite and the skipper had nursed her all the way; we were nearly home." His arm dropped back into his lap and he was silent for a moment, memories flooding back. "But," he continued finally, his voice little more than a whisper, "the damn rudder decided to fall off." He shook his head. "Even a Lancaster can't fly without a rudder."

As they held mine, old Arthur's eyes, just for that moment, lost the mischievous sparkle and became deep, dark pools of sadness. I felt myself drawn to that day, that perilous moment. "So what happened...? How did you...?"

"The skipper ordered us out," the old man continued. "I was the first to go and as I left, Romeo Victor went into a violent spin." He heaved a heavy sigh. "They never stood a chance. Twenty-one missions," he muttered, almost to himself. "Same crew, twenty-one missions. Brothers, we were. Always together. Always." His voice had dropped to a whisper. "But it all went wrong that day, lad. You see, they went without me. They didn't mean to, couldn't help themselves, but they did. They went without me."

~ * ~

We've been here for three years now and we couldn't be happier, every year better than the last. It's winter now and as I stand looking out of the window, a roaring fire in the grate, the surrounding fields, covered with a light dusting of snow, look as beautiful as ever.

Earlier this year, September the twelfth it was, I remember it well because it was the day before my birthday. It was also the day Arthur "Chalky" White died. He was ninety-two and as they lowered him into the ground, I was there at the graveside. As the coffin came to rest something tugged my eyes sideways, toward a raised hillock beyond the adjacent field. Bathed in the red glow of a softening September sunset lounged a small group of young men. My heart skipped and I looked around at the other mourners. Nobody else was looking that way. Most had their heads bowed, listening to the vicar's last words. But they were there, honestly, I can assure you, all six of them. They were too far away for me to see the expressions on their faces, but I would have wagered anything they were all smiling. Well they would be, wouldn't they? They had waited for their comrade for a very long time and now all seven would be together again. And I'm sure wherever they went from there they would stay that way.

No, I'm like you; I don't believe in ghosts either. When your time's up it's up, finished, right?

Yeah, well like I said…maybe.

# COWARDY CUSTARD

I feel the needle enter my flesh. No pain, just a slight stinging sensation followed by a pleasant warmth creeping up my arm. I've no idea what they're putting into me, what it's called, and I don't care. I know only very soon the pain will ebb and, for a short time anyway, I will feel more comfortable.

"How's that?" The voice, feminine and caring, comes together with a gentle massaging at the needle's point of entry.

"Better, I hope," I mumble, my lips taught and painful.

"Give it a few minutes," the voice soothes. "It'll soon start to work." The massaging stops but the hand remains, resting comfortingly warm on my arm. "Do you need anything else?"

I shake my head tentatively from side to side. "I don't think so. Unless you can remove these damned bandages. Then at least I could see what you look like." My own words kindle dark thoughts. "That's if I'm still able to see."

The hand, still on my arm, a gentle pressure. "Don't be silly now. The doctor will see you this afternoon. He'll have the bandages off in no time. You'll be fine, you'll see." The voice gives a soft little chuckle. "And you're not missing anything by not being able to see me, I can assure you." The hand leaves my arm, its comforting warmth missed immediately.

"Don't forget the button if you need me."

"Nurse?"

"Yes."

"How's Tim?"

An awkward silence and for a moment I think she's left me.

"Nurse?"

"As soon as I hear anything, you'll be the first to know. I promise."

I listen to her footsteps tap businesslike away and roll the plastic pushbutton between my fingers, comforted in the knowledge a single push will bring her back to my bedside.

And as she promised, the pain slowly subsides. It doesn't go away; it never has yet, not completely. But it diminishes enough for stressed, taught muscles to relax just a little; for shallow, tight breathing to slow. I feel myself drifting into a semiconscious state. My mind, as if on a slowly moving swing, seesawing back and forth between past and present.

"Cowardy, cowardy custard, can't cut the mustard." The words ring stridently clear. I totter precariously on top of the narrow brick wall, the all too familiar terror creeping into the back of my throat, hot tears burning my eyes. I look across at the branch, no more than two feet from me. Close, so close and yet…

Young voices scream from below. "Go on jump. Tim can, Tim can do it."

My heart pounds. I look down at the upturned faces lining the wall. Grinning, expectant faces; faces that know whatever they call me, however hard they shout, in the end it will be of no use. And as if acknowledging this, the faces distort and dissolve into a pool of darkness.

I feel for the reassurance of the pushbutton in my hand again, the plastic sticking to my sweaty palm. I hear sounds; footsteps, the rustling of starched fabric passing, murmurings, a muted, comforting female laugh.

I breathe deeply, an attempt to slow a racing heart. My tongue sticks to the roof of a dry, raw mouth. I should take a drink. But I can't, not now. Not now that Tim has the wheel.

"For Christ sake, Tim, slow down."

He turns to me, gleaming, joy filled eyes perilously leaving the road ahead. "Nothing to worry about, Mike, you're safe with me, old son." Safe with me. Safe with me. The words echo on and on.

I can feel myself gripping the corner of the seat. The same fear as all those years before scorching the back of my throat.

"But the road's slippery, Tim. The road's icy and you're going too bloody fast. Can't you see that? Can't you understand what I'm telling you?"

Clear, outrageously blue eyes hold mine, ignoring the narrow road screaming toward us, ignoring my plea. "God, Mike, you are such a wimp, always were such a wimp."

"Tim, for goodness sake listen." I try to shout, but hear only my own words mumbled through painful lips. The terrifying road ahead evaporates and I drift back into confused consciousness.

Slowly, carefully I reach sideways, searching, painful fingers, lucky, finding the glass. I gulp gratefully, the water washing the stinging bile from the back of my throat. Still clasping the glass, I let my head fall back onto a chilled, sweat dampened pillow.

"Cowardy, cowardy custard." The taunt any ten year old boy would dread. It was simple; climb the wall, leap to the branch, swing happily to and fro a few times and drop to the ground. They all did it. And Tim first, always first, the leader. Tim did everything first; the more difficult, the more dangerous, the better. There were other things, too. Things they all dared to do. Things, in Tim's presence, none of them would dare not do. It was only me that couldn't. Only me, Tim's cowardy, cowardy custard little brother, that couldn't.

"You're just different, that's all." Mother hugs me to her, kissing the top of my head, knowing me for what I am and conscious of my suffering. And a true mother, always trying to make it better. "You can't be the same as Tim. Brothers are never the same. Tim is physical, always has been. You're the brainy one. Just wait until you're older, you'll see." But the comfort only lasted until the next time and after all those years, until this time.

Status Quo roars at us from the CD player. Tim sings happily along.

"Too fast, Tim, much too fast. Look, Tim, for God's sake look. Trees straight ahead. The bend, it's too tight." Now, only now does he look, the smile fading, fingers tightening on the steering wheel. Now he knows. Now he realizes.

"Oh Tim, you fool, you crazy, bloody fool."

Petrol. The smell fills my nostrils. My stomach turns and I retch violently, my chest irrupting in painful spasm. But what, where, how? I drag myself onto one elbow, crying out as the pain, such vicious pain, again cuts through my side. Blurred vision slowly clears and I'm looking down. A steep, tree-covered slope. The petrol, ever stronger, clogs my throat. What's happened? Think, damn you think. Slowly it returns. Tim, the road, the pounding of Status Quo. That's it, the car. But where the hell is the car?

It's not loud; not a bang, not like an explosion. No, more like a gasp, a gentle whoosh, but I know, instinctively I know what it is.

"Tim." I frantically call to my brother, but the pain in my side sucks the breath from me, cutting the word to no more than a hoarse whisper.

I look down, searching. Then I see it. Nose down, maybe twenty feet below, the passenger door hanging shattered from its hinges, smoke oozing from beneath the bonnet and now, that instantly recognizable sound, tiny yellow flames licking from around one crushed front wheel. I

44

shake my head, not understanding. The car far below and me, here, twenty feet above, how can that be? It takes precious seconds, but slowly the obvious dawns; the open passenger door, I must have been thrown clear.

But Tim, what about Tim? Was he still in the car? I drag myself closer to the edge, clinging petrified as I peer down the precarious, almost vertical slope. My heart stops as my pain filled, terrified brain comprehends the crumpled, broken shape jammed over the steering wheel.

I look frantically around. I need help, there has to be someone, anyone. But there is no one. There is only me. My breath comes in short gasps as I watch the slowly increasing flames continue to lick around the front of the car. My eyes scan the trees growing from the side of the slope, the branches, my only path to the stricken car and my doomed brother. To my horror my only option becomes clear and I drag myself painfully to a sitting position, my legs dangling over the edge. For what seems an eternity I stare at the first branch. It's no more than two feet from me.

"Cowardy, cowardy, custard, can't cut the mustard. Cowardy, cowardy..."

I launch myself toward the branch, unbelievable pain scything through my chest. I scream.

"Mister Harris. Michael."

Firm fingers gently pry the pushbutton from within my tightly clenched fist. "You were dreaming. Just a bad dream, that's all," the now familiar voice soothes. "You almost crushed your caller."

"Sorry," I croak, my mouth tinder dry. I try to heave myself into a more comfortable position and gasp.

Restraining hands hold my shoulders. "Don't try to lift yourself," she warns. "Broken ribs don't take kindly to it." Her strong hands gently ease me up. "Better?"

"Yes, thank you."

"You have a visitor."

The sound of a chair being pulled to the bedside. A presence, warm and close. A familiar perfume.

"Hello, Michael." Jane, Tim's beautiful wife, the soft, husky voice instantly recognizable.

"Hello, Jane."

"How are you?"

Scorched lips bring an instant end to an attempted smile. "They say I'll live. How's Tim?"

"He's knocked about a bit." Clipped, restrained words, an attempt to lighten the moment, maybe for my benefit. "They say it's too early to tell yet. But he's alive, Michael, so fingers crossed eh?" The last few words stutter to a close, her composure cracking.

"Yeah, fingers crossed," I repeat quickly to cover her break. I'm happy to let the silence that follows linger, give her a chance to collect herself.

"They told me what you did, Michael," she says finally, her voice little more than a whisper. "You pulled him from that car; you got him out. They say they don't know how you did it; you were so badly hurt yourself. But you did, Michael, despite the fire, the explosion. And now you're burned and your eyes, maybe even…" Again the emotional hic in her voice, the words tumbling into silence.

"Yeah, well," I mumble. Two meaningless words, but all I can muster.

"If he pulls through, Michael, he'll owe you everything. He'll owe you his life."

I hear her grateful words and hope with all my heart my brother does pull through. But even now, even knowing my own injuries could ruin my life, I think about a terrible demon that has at last been laid to rest. I reach out and feel her gently take my hand.

"He owes me nothing, Jane," I tell her, my heart lifting. "In fact, if anything, I owe him."

# BUT I HATE BOATS

"A sea trip?"

"Yes."

"The real sea, with waves and all?"

"Yes, the real sea, but there don't have to be waves. Well, not big ones anyway."

"But, I hate boats. You know I hate boats."

The others grinned.

I sighed.

I knew it. As soon as the guy mentioned boats, I knew I had a problem.

I'd known Benny since we were kids. We grew up together. In the late fifties we'd formed our first band together, played together ever since. We'd always been close, our interests the same. Except Benny was a confirmed bachelor. He'd had plenty of opportunities, of course, but he had never wanted to be tied down. Women always came second to his music. There wasn't much we didn't know about each other and I certainly knew about Benny and boats. I knew what was coming next, too. I could hear it now. "They keep going up and down, blah, blah, blah…"

"They keep going up and down, don't they?" he whined. "Never keep still. You know what'll happen. I'll end up yackin' in someone's lap."

There, I knew he'd say it. The others giggled.

I gritted my teeth.

Okay, so there had been the unfortunate incident during that trip off Brighton pier. And, yes, he had been sick down the front of the unfortunate lady's dress. But that was the only time. All the other times he had managed to get to the side of the boat. Well, apart from the time in the rowing boat on the Battersea park lake. They weren't my best trousers anyway and they washed out okay.

I scanned the five of them, sitting round the pub table, their pints in front of them. Including myself, a combined age of over three hundred years. Four grinning like aged, delinquent Cheshire Cats, Benny looking miserable.

"Look," I said, as patiently as I could. "They're celebrating the town's refurbished pier with a short boat trip. They want a jazz band on board. We don't get many gigs these days, and it's only a three hour trip. The fee is far better than we usually get, that's when we get any fee at all, and all the grub and booze is free. What more could you want?"

Benny stared sadly into his pint. "But I do hate boats," he whined.

The others spluttered in their beers.

I dropped my head into my hands.

The pills had swung it, just. The Pharmacist, I told Benny, had guaranteed they would work. Okay, he actually said he couldn't guarantee it, but they generally worked...on some people.

So I'd stretched the truth a bit, but at least it did the trick. Benny had swallowed the line and the pills. He'd agreed to go.

We arrived early and parked directly outside the pier entrance. It was a long pier and the boat--I was glad to see it was large; we were told it carried two hundred--was moored at the far end. From somewhere they'd found us a trolley to carry our gear. It was a big, heavy trolley and they hadn't found anyone to push it.

We were half way there when Fred, our banjo player, and a twenty a day man for the last forty years, was in trouble. "God," he gasped. "I don't mind boats; in fact I like boats. I hate trolleys, though. I really hate trolleys. Anyone got a ciggie?"

Arthur, our trumpet player, also exhausted, giggled uncontrollably and sunk to his knees. Benny stared apprehensively at the boat sitting at the end of the pier. The rest of us clung to the now stationary trolley for support.

Two fit looking youngsters trotted across. One helped Arthur to his feet, the other turned to me. "Give you a push, pop," he said cheerfully.

Like Fred, I don't mind boats. Truth is, I don't mind trolleys, either. But I do hate being called pop by kids.

The organiser and pier manager was probably in his late thirty's. He had flowing blond hair arranged carefully and was very cheerful. We thought, after pushing a loaded trolley for half a mile, a bit too cheerful.

He ushered us toward a small area at the end of the lower deck. "This is where you play, chaps," he prattled. The hair, casually flicked to one side, immediately dropped perfectly back into place. "If there is anything at all you need, just call me" He bustled off, stopping and turning after a few paces. "It's Gilbert, by the way. Anything at all, just call for Gilbert. They all do." With another flick of his head he was gone.

"Need a fag," said Fred, leaning exhausted against the rail, his hands frantically searching his pockets.

"Me too," I said, holding out my hand.

"It's moving; can you feel it," whispered Benny. "Where's the toilet, I'd better find where the toilet is." He noticed my raised eyes. "Well, y'know. Better safe than sorry, eh?"

The others grinned.

I sighed. "Don't start," I begged. "You know what the guy said; those pills are infallible, right?" Benny wasn't convinced.

49

It was a soft, balmy summers evening with just a gentle swell and we left the pier at exactly seven. Gilbert would have it no other way, of course. As well as the Mayor, the passengers included the businessmen who had supported the pier refurbishment. Gilbert flitted between them ensuring all was well. His permanently painted smile grew even wider when he heard me announce our first number to be "Over the waves". He gave us the thumbs up on that. Benny, his face already a little pale, didn't agree.

I have to admit, Benny did okay. Well, for the first hour, anyway. Tentative, but okay. In fact there was a time when he even seemed to be enjoying it. But during our first break he stood at the rail with Fred looking out to sea. Big mistake!

"Where the hell is he?" I hissed. We were due to start the second set and there was no sign of Benny.

"Dunno," said Fred. "One minute I was talking to him, the next..." He shrugged his shoulders. "Gone for a pee, I expect."

We had done it before and a cornet and clarinet are a good combination, but a two-man front line is a bit thin. Gilbert noticed after only our second number.

"What's happened, chaps," he fussed, his concerned words accompanied by the habitual flick of the head, the wispy hair doing its usual circuit before falling back exactly where it had started. "Where's your friend?"

The others tittered.

I bit my lip. "He's, er... He's not feeling too good."

"Oh, my dear chap, nothing serious, I hope."

"Seasick," piped up Arthur, gleefully. "He gets seasick."

I glared. Thanks a bunch, Art'. Not stomach ache, or even headache. Oh no, not our Arthur. "Er...Yes," I mumbled feebly. "Just a slight case. He'll be fine shortly."

"Seasick," Gilbert crowed. "Seasick. My dear chap, you are very naughty." The flick seemed more exaggerated than ever. "Didn't I say any problems call Gilbert? Didn't I say that?" He swung around and surveyed the passengers around him. After a few seconds he waved his hand and called across the deck. "Miranda, darling, over here, please."

I looked at Fred who silently mouthed "Miranda?"

I shrugged.

She was, I guess, in her fifties and looked every bit the sailor with a dark blue cap at a jaunty angle over hair cut as short as a man. A blue denim shirt, sleeves rolled almost to the elbows of muscular arms, was tucked into tight fitting blue jeans beneath which protruded a well-worn pair of deck shoes. Miranda didn't walk; she rolled across the deck toward us.

"Chaps," said Gilbert, with a flick "this is Miranda."

I smiled and offered my hand. "Nice to meet you, Miranda."

She gripped my hand. "Likewise," was all she said and I wondered if I would ever play the clarinet again.

Gilbert, appearing not to notice my tortured expression, draped an arm around Miranda's shoulder and whispered for some seconds into her ear. As he did so a grin spread across her face. Finally, nodding, she simply said "Roger" and rolled off across the deck.

Gilbert turned back to us, this time with a triumphant flick. "Play on, chaps," he said, rubbing his hands together expressively. "Your man will be back with you in a jiffy."

And he was. Barely had we finished the next number when Benny strode across the deck toward us, still pale but a wide grin on his face, a brimming pint in his hand.

"Right," he said, pulling his trombone off its stand. "What's next?"

I caught Fred's raised eyebrows and shrugged again.

"Alright?" I asked Benny.

He looked surprised. "Why wouldn't I be?"

"Well...I thought you weren't feeling too good."

"Me? Never." He looked around at the others, a puzzled expression on his face. "What're you bozos looking at," he asked. Then turning back to me. "What're they looking at?"

"Nothing, Ben," I said quickly. "Let's get on with it, shall we?"

Benny worked the slide of his trombone vigorously. "'Bout time," he said. "Wait all day for you lazy lot."

The others stared, open mouthed.

So did I.

It was a couple of weeks after the boat trip when he phoned. "Like to talk; got something to ask you," he said. We agreed to meet.

His car was already in the pub car park when I arrived. Unusual for Benny; he was late for everything. I pushed through the bar door and stopped dead. There she was, pint in hand, cap at a jaunty angle. And there he was, pint in hand and...cap, yellow!, also at a jaunty angle. I approached cautiously.

"Ben?" Was all I could muster.

"I wanted you to be the first to know," he said coyly. "We're getting married. Next week. Want you to be best man." He turned his head and their eyes locked. It was my turn to feel nauseous.

As though Benny had lost the power of speech Miranda took over. "Next Thursday," she said grasping his spare hand lovingly. He showed no indication of pain. "The honeymoon starts on Saturday; a two week cruise."

"Best man? Yes, of course," I stammered. "But Ben, a cruise? You hate...I mean, boats...the sea." I pulled out my cigarettes, lit up and dragged deeply. "You hate boats."

Benny said nothing. He just smiled stupidly and sipped his pint. She reached into the back pocket of her jeans, "You know, smoking is so bad for your health," she said, handing me a small business card. "You should really try to quit."

I watched Ben gaze lovingly into her eyes before looking down at the card.

Smoking? Bad habits? Phobias?

Visit Miranda and try hypnosis.

It really does work.

# VICTIM

He thought the speedometer showed 80mph but he couldn't be sure. He was having trouble focusing, his eyes continuously drawn to the strobing blue light filling the rear view mirror. His heart leaped as he looked back to the road and saw the grass verge slicing toward him. Cursing violently, he yanked at the steering wheel. The car swayed violently back and forth before settling again into a straight line. He knew he must concentrate, but his hands, sticky with sweat, were finding it difficult to keep control and the cramp in his stomach and the ever-increasing bouts of shaking made it almost impossible. A roundabout suddenly appeared and again the car swung sickeningly from side to side as he clumsily forced it round, seeing the slip road to the motorway only just in time. A sigh of relief broke from his lips at the sight of the straight road now stretching before him and the car surged forward as he punched his foot hard on the accelerator. He didn't know where the road would take him; miles back he had lost all sense of direction, but if he could just lose the car behind.

He'd had no intention of taking the car; he hadn't even expected it to be unlocked. He was just doing as he always did, trying each car and hoping. Hoping as always to find an unlocked car with something worthwhile inside. It was just one of the ways he was able to keep

54

himself supplied. But people were becoming much more aware and unlocked cars were becoming rare. Unlike his need which was ever increasing.

Surprised as he was to find the BMW unlocked, he'd been quick to take advantage. Grabbing a bag carelessly thrown onto the passenger seat, he was about to leave the car when he'd seen the keys hanging from the ignition. There was just a second's hesitation. He'd never stolen a car before, how would he dispose of it? But he had the keys and what might be in the boot? If he just drove the car to a quiet spot, he would have all the time in the world to search it and take whatever he wanted. Before he knew it he was driving the car away. He'd felt elated, a real score. But his elation had been short lived. The police car had appeared behind him only minutes later.

He was twenty-two years old. He might have been forty. Although almost six foot, the ragged clothes he wore hung loosely on his thin unkempt frame. He couldn't remember when it had started. Now, like every other memory, it was lost in a timeless mist. Had his brain not been addled he would have recalled the day when he had been met outside the school gates. He had known the lad; he was just a few years older than him and had attended the school; he laughingly called himself one of the old brigade. That day they had walked part of the way home together, the lad telling him how much fun he was always having and how good life was. The exams were coming up, weren't they? And he wanted to pass, didn't he? Get good results, get a good job? He had been so confident, so sure. Why not take a couple of the tablets, free gratis, just to see how he got on with them. Then if he ever wanted any more...

It had been over eighteen months before his mother had become suspicious, and by that time he had graduated beyond those few simple tablets. The inevitable showdown with his parents had been the most miserable moment of his life. But even confronted with the irrefutable evidence found in his bedroom, he still denied it vehemently. It belonged to a friend, he had argued, he was just looking after it.

"You can lead a horse to water, but you can't make it drink," the manager at the rehabilitation centre had said. "He has got to want to kick the habit beyond all else. If he doesn't, we can't help him." He remembered the three pairs of eyes boring into him, his mother's imploring, begging. For her sake he had confirmed he really did, beyond all else, want to kick the habit. He was very convincing and they had believed him. He wished he had believed himself.

They had led the horse to water, but try as it might, it could not drink. The day he had walked out, he had said for some fresh air in the gardens, he knew he was never going back. He had arrived in London with a just few pounds in his pocket, the clothes on his back, and an address written on a scruffy piece of paper.

He'd stood in front of the door of the small house in the grubby back street and double-checked the number before ringing the bell. It was some minutes before there was any sign of life then the door opened just a crack. A few more seconds elapsed before the door was fully opened revealing a tall thickset young man in jeans and sweat stained T-shirt. "Well, well look who's here," he'd said with a wide grin. "Long time no see, eh?" He was right; it had been some time since they last met outside the school gates.

He made new friends and through them, on the London streets, drifted into a new way of life. He was surprised, after being taught the ropes, just how easy shoplifting and house breaking was. And there were always cash paying customers for the right goods. The trying of car door handles in search of the absentminded car owner had become routine. He existed from day to day and thought of little more than his visits to the scruffy little house to spend the proceeds from his petty crimes.

Only once, after the theft of a woman's surprisingly full purse from her shopping basket outside a supermarket, did he ever decide to visit his mother. An early morning train delivered him to the station just a couple of streets away from his village home just outside London. He waited until his father, looking older and more stooped than he remembered, left for work.

Recognition of the sorry looking individual before her had taken a few seconds then, with a sob, his mother fell on him, clutching him to her. He'd tried to respond by wrapping his arms about her, but he somehow felt remote and despite the familiar surroundings it was as if he were a stranger in this place. His mother had ushered him in to the house, all the time plying him with questions, running her fingers through the long hair that fell matted before his eyes. Sitting in the lounge where he had happily sat in complete contentment so many times during his early years he had smelled the clean, familiar smell of his home. Familiar and yet alien.

She had cooked him food, plied him with endless cups of tea and talked incessantly, begging him to come home, promising to look after him, to solve all his problems. Her love and devotion shone through tear filled eyes and deep down he knew he should be feeling something, something of the love that had been before. But his drug-saturated body was anaesthetized from all emotion and there was nothing. He knew then he should not have come. He didn't belong here anymore. There was an urge to get away, to be free from his mother's suffocating presence and to be back with his own kind.

He'd noticed the handbag on the hall table as he had come in. It had registered, not as his mother's, but simply as another source of income. He asked if he could have another cup of tea and while his mother, eager to please, was in the kitchen he slipped into the hall, removed the purse from the handbag and quietly slipped out the front door.

He sat on the train, a huge grin across his face. The purse had yielded twenty-five pounds; success indeed. He glanced disinterestedly at the other contents of the purse, including treasured photographs of his father and himself as a child, before carelessly throwing it out of the train window. He knew he would never return and as he looked forward to his next visit to the scruffy little house in the back streets of London, his mother was already becoming a vague memory.

~ * ~

They estimated the BMW had been travelling at approximately 95mph when it veered to the left and hit the concrete upright of the motorway flyover, the pursuing police car lucky not to be involved in the accident.

The crushed body found in the car was that of a young man, though at first he was thought to be much older. He carried no identification and the post mortem revealed a very high level of hard drugs in the blood.

The owner of the BMW was sad at its loss, but duly filled in his insurance claim and was, in due course, reimbursed. The police inspector in charge of the case noted the verdict of "Death by Misadventure" and felt lucky to have one less criminal to deal with on his patch. With the memory of the crumpled figure dragged from wrecked car still vivid in his mind, he also thought thankfully of his own two happy healthy sons.

A sad little lady in a house in a London suburb couldn't bring herself to tell her husband of their son's visit. She did tell him about the loss of her purse, though, and he bought her a nice new leather one. She said she was pleased, but he did wonder why it made her cry so.

# THE BEST LAID PLANS

I spread the diagram out on the table. It was rough, hand drawn, but as far as I could remember accurate with all the necessary details, everything we needed.

"Ok, Ken," I say. "Let's go through it one more time, just to be sure."

Ken nodded enthusiastically. "Yeah, Bri'. We don't want any mistakes this time, do we?"

I eyeballed him across the table. "No, Ken, no mistakes this time."

We've been mates all our lives, Ken and me. Brought up together, we were. Lived next door to each other since we were born, me just one day ahead of Ken. Our mums and dads are best mates too, so I suppose you could say we were more like brothers than neighbours. You know, in and out of each other's houses all the time. Mum used to say, "Brian, you should knock a hole through that wall. That way you two boys wouldn't have to keep going out of one front door and in the other." She was right too, but we never did.

I remember when Ken and me started school. Again on the same day. Still got the photo; two little lads hand in hand, eager to get amongst it. Years later, we got expelled on the same day too. Can't say I've got a photo of that, but it's funny how sometimes two people's lives run in parallel isn't it?

And they say like father like son, don't they? Well that's certainly the case with Ken and me. You see our dads were always involved in...how can I put it? Well mum used to say the only way they could have got better known to the police was by joining the force. Bit unfair, that, but you get the idea, don't you? Mind you, there was never anything heavy. No violence or anything like that. And Ken and me, we're the same. It sort of runs in our families, like a natural progression. Like I said, like father like son.

I looked back down at the drawing. "Now we know the only day we can do it is on the Thursday, right?"

Ken nodded. "Right, Bri', on a Thursday." He hesitated, his brow wrinkled. "Er, why was that again, Bri'?"

Now you might have already gathered Ken isn't the sharpest knife in the drawer. But what you have to understand is he is honest--if I can put it that way--and loyal. The best way to explain Ken is he is a doer, not a thinker. As long as he knows what he has to do, he's fine. And when working, I'd rather have him alongside me than anyone else I know. It's just sometimes it takes a while for things to click. Mind you, once he's got it, he never forgets. Well almost never anyway.

I reminded him. "We're not quite sure why, but Thursday is the one day when their business hours get out of kilter with the bank, remember? It's the last Thursday in the month. The only day when they have to hold the money on the premises overnight."

Ken's face cleared. "Right, gotcha, Bri'. Fifty grand." He licked his lips.

"Yeah, that's what Lennie the Lip gave out. As near as makes no odds to fifty thousand smackers sitting there all night."

"That's it, good old Lennie. He should know, shouldn't he, Bri'?"

"That he should, Ken boy. After all, he worked there, didn't he?"

I should mention here Lennie Harris, or Lennie the Lip as he is affectionately known on the street--on account of his ability to give out any information required to facilitate a job--is another of our associates. Lenny is always a very handy person to have around. Sometimes even essential, as in this current situation when he actually worked at the establishment in question. I say *worked* as opposed to *works* because having divulged certain sensitive information regarding his employer, particularly information that could lead to a slight loss in that employer's finances, Lennie felt it best to terminate his employment in advance of that loss, thereby lessening the possibility of him being accused of any involvement. We all agreed this to be a wise precaution.

Now you could say Lennie would be disadvantaged by this loss of earnings, but you see it's all about swings and roundabouts. Lennie loses a weekly salary, but despite not actually taking part in our little escapade, actually gains because of it. You see Lonnie's fee varies from job to job depending on the level of information given out. In this case it was twenty percent of the take, which Ken and me figured to be fair seeing as he had not only given us the appropriate day to operate, but also the very layout of the gaff in question. We agreed that was worth twenty percent and no mistake, right? And anyway, Lennie could always get another job.

"So we know it has to be a Thursday," I say, reverting back to the drawing.

Ken nods his agreement.

"So first things first. The car."

"Yup, no prob's, Bri'. Bog standard, run of the mill. Nothing fancy, nothing that stands out."

"You got it, Ken boy. So what then?"

"Vauxhall Astra, dark blue, Bri'. Loads of 'em about. Easy to get."

"And where do you get it?"

"Long stay car park. With a bit of luck it won't be missed for some time."

See what I mean? Once he's got it, he's fine.

"Okay, so we leave it till after midnight before we go in," I say. "You drop me round the back of the building and I go in here." We both peer down at the drawing to where my fingertip rests. "Then I'll need at least an hour."

"One hour," Ken repeats. I could see his brain working furiously to log and retain the information.

"Yeah, an hour. I need that long," I explain slowly, "because I have to disconnect the alarm system, get through the back door and two inner doors then crack the safe."

Now all of what I have just explained to Ken might, to the uninitiated, seem a bit of a tall order. But, as I explained earlier, like father, like son. Dad, before his enforced retirement--enforced by mum, that is. She said that if she had wanted to spend half her life talking to herself, she would have joined a nunnery--was the best peterman of his day. And he took great joy in passing on his skills to his only son. So, in most cases, locked doors gave me no problems whatsoever. A safe, too, provided it was a make with which I was familiar, and Lennie the Lip assured me it was, was also a doddle.

"Now this is important, Ken," I continue. "If I'm finished earlier, I'll wait in the shadow of the doorway."

"Shadow of doorway, Bri'," he repeats.

"Yeah. And if it takes longer, you'll have to come back."

"Come back?" The puzzled frown again.

"Don't forget after you drop me off you'll have to make yourself scarce, maybe cruise around or park up somewhere inconspicuous. Can't have you sitting outside the place at that time in the morning, can we? Some nosy insomniac is bound to spot you, right?"

"Oh yeah, 'course, the insomni-thing, Bri. I remember now. Find somewhere to park up. Somewhere safe."

"Good lad. Okay, so now let's go through my bit, just to be sure I haven't forgotten anything."

We had been over it so many times I knew it by heart. But sometimes, no matter how hard you try, how many times you go through it all, cover every angle, things can still go pear shaped, can't they?

Anyway, before I was able to open my mouth and continue, the lights went out and we found ourselves in semi-darkness, the only light now being the rays of a watery moon filtering through the little window. I sighed and folded up the plan.

"No use going on if we can't see the plan, Ken," I say. "Best give it a rest tonight and go over it again tomorrow. We've got lots of time now."

"Yeah, lots of time now, Bri'." Ken moved across the room and stretched out on his bed. "It was getting a bit complicated again anyway, wasn't it, Bri'?"

I flopped down onto my own bed and lay staring at the ceiling, churning things over in my mind. It was a good plan, no doubt about that. And fifty thousand pounds, I mean fifty thousand. Even without Lonnie's twenty per cent we would still have got…well, we'd still have got a lot. Don't think dad would have ever made that much. I thought about dad and his enforced retirement. Mum would make sure it started in a few weeks' time. As soon as he got out, that was. She said Tim and me should retire too. I promised her I'd think about it and the way things have gone recently, it might not be such a bad idea.

Unable to sleep, I prop myself up on a pillow and light a cigarette. "Ken."

"Yeah, Bri'."

"The car."

"Dark blue Astra, Bri'?"

"Yeah, the Astra. Tell me again where you parked up."

"Supermarket car park. Right at the back, Bri'. Out of sight."

"Then what happened again?"

"I noticed me watch had stopped, Bri'."

"And tell me again. Why did you stop the police car and ask them the time?"

"Well I forgot about the clock on the Astra's dash, Bri' and at that time in the morning there was no one else about, was there? You did say an hour, Bri', and I didn't want to let you down, did I?"

Like I said, Ken's not the sharpest knife in the drawer, but hey, we've been best mates all our lives. I think we'll run through it just once more tomorrow, cover all the angles again. After all, like I said, we've got plenty of time and there's nothing else to do. Although I'm pretty sure I know where things went wrong now.

"'Night, Ken."

"'Night, Bri'"

"Bri'?"

"Yes, Ken."

"Nice of 'em to put us in the same cell."

"Yeah, very nice, Ken."

"Bri'"

"Yes, Ken."

"Think we might wangle Lennie in here too?"

"'Night, Ken."

# IT'S A SHED

"But we've already got a shed."

"What?" She looked up from the picture, a frown creasing her forehead.

"A shed," I repeated, pointing down at the open page. "We've already got a shed."

"It is not a shed," she said, running her finger along the caption. "Look, it says summerhouse. It's a summerhouse, their latest design."

I should have noted the warning signs. The tight lips, the sudden flash in her eyes, heaven knows we've been married long enough. But honestly, it was so obvious; it was a shed, wasn't it? Oh, a fancy one, no doubt, but a shed nonetheless.

"It might be their latest design," I persisted, "but it's still a shed."

She looked at me long and hard, her forefinger gently tracing a line back and forth across those tight lips. That was another sign. "No, a shed is what you have," she said finally, a strained, but for the moment, patient edge to her words. "Where you keep your garden tools. You know, those things you never go near."

I tried to ignore the dig. It's true; gardening is not my favourite pastime. In fact, as she well knows, I hate it and will do anything to distance myself from it. Gardening, in my opinion, is a never ending drudgery of unnecessary effort, dirty hands and results that last almost no time at all. Take grass cutting as an example. Though probably the lesser of all gardening evils, it's still a total waste of time. No sooner is the mower stowed safely in the shed than it has to be dragged out again. No, definitely not my scene. I see myself more as the sophisticated, indoor type. A comfortable chair, a good book, the occasional single malt at my elbow. Mind you I'm not totally against the outdoors, it has its benefits-- sometimes. For instance, on a fine Sunday morning there is nothing better than enjoying a pint in the beer garden of the Dog and Duck. In the fine weather, of course. George--he's our next door neighbour and good friend--and I often indulge ourselves there, though it's not always appreciated by you know who. But as I see it, a man needs some relaxation time.

The shed, my shed, was purchased some years before. That was her idea too. At first I wasn't keen, but as it turned out it came to suit me just fine. At the bottom of the garden, behind some bushes--she calls them flowering shrubs I believe--the tools, clean and tidy, tucked neatly away out of sight, out of mind. Most of the time it works well. Though I do, as now, have to suffer the occasional jibe. You see, the garden is the love of her life and she doesn't understand why I can't share her enthusiasm. Earlier in our marriage I did try, but over the years, she has grudgingly had to accept, garden-wise, I am more of a hindrance than a help. You see, not knowing a daffodil from a bird bath, I always manage to tread on or break off some rare, treasured specimen. Purely accidental, you understand, but as a result, on the odd occasion I do venture through the back door, I am generally restricted to the patio where I can do little damage. I am very occasionally requested to mow the lawn, but only when WI duty calls and time is short. And always under strict instruction to keep my feet firmly on the grassed area. She is convinced, and with some justification I have to admit, that should I stray from there, it is inevitable that another of those treasured specimens would be bound to meet its end. And I'm happy with that. As I've already said, cutting the grass being the least of all gardening chores, an hour strolling behind the mower is just about acceptable. But this latest fad, a fancy shed. What new dangers lurked there? Could it unsettle a long standing status quo, I wondered?

I looked again at the picture. "Okay, so it's not a shed, it's a summerhouse. But what does it do?"

"Do? It doesn't *do* anything. It's a feature, it enhances the garden."

"You just look at it then."

"No, you don't just look at it," she growled. "You use it."

"For what?"

"To relax in. It's another way of enjoying the garden."

"You mean you sit in it?"

"Yes…er no. Well sort of. In and out of it."

I frowned, shaking my head. "In *and* out of it? Sorry, I don't quite understand…"

"On its little veranda," she said agitatedly. "In one of the garden chairs. On a nice day, for instance. A cup of tea, out in the fresh air, enjoying looking at the fruits of your labour."

A little shiver ran through me. "Fruits of labour. On a nice day?"

She nodded.

"Like a nice, sunny Sunday morning?"

"If you like."

There it was. There was the hidden danger. Sunday morning, drinking tea outside a shed. An instant picture of the Dog and Duck slowly diminishing into infinity formed in my mind. I shifted uncomfortably in my chair. "But we can sit drinking tea on the patio," I protested feebly. Last year we bought all that expensive patio furniture…"

"No," she interrupted. "I want the summerhouse at the bottom of the garden. It will give an entirely different aspect to everything."

Another shiver. "You mean at the bottom, on the left, under the trees?"

She nodded. "It will enable us to look back at the house. We never do that now."

It will also give a clear view of my shed, I thought, and a constant reminder of the unused tools sitting clean and comfortably locked away inside. I could picture the scene now, hear the words. Between thoughtful sips of tea, her eyes wandering to the previously hidden shed. "You should use your garden tools more often, you know. I'm sure if you spent more time in the garden you would grow to love it as much as I do."

Wrong. More time in the garden would only make me hate it more. I thought for a moment, considering a different tack. "So if we only sit on the little veranda, what happens inside the she..., er the summerhouse?"

"Well, there would be a little table and a couple of chairs. Maybe curtains and a few plants."

"Plants? What about the expensive greenhouse we bought the year before last? I thought plants was what the greenhouse was all about."

"No, no," she sighed, the dreaded condescending smile appearing. "I don't mean growing plants, I mean decorative, flowering plants. In pots, in the windows."

"Oh." I began to feel the argument slipping away. I wasn't surprised. It always did.

Most times I didn't mind, but this was different. This drew me into the depths of the garden, my worst nightmare and worse still it threatened Sunday mornings and the Dog and Duck. I dug deep. Maybe just one last try. "You know sheds get infested with spiders," I ventured, knowing her fear of all six legged creatures.

Her eyes narrowed. "Not if you regularly clean it out," she hissed through gritted teeth. "And for the hundredth time it is *not* a shed, it's a summerhouse."

D'you know, we've been married for forty years now and there are those who would say it's a perfect partnership. Certainly I have nothing to complain about. I couldn't have asked for a more steadfast, loyal and loving partner. I should probably add pedantic to that list, but nonetheless steadfast, loyal and loving. In the past, I have even been asked what I thought was the most important factor to maintaining a close, long term relationship. My answer was, and always will be, the same. Knowing what your partner really wants, and if at all possible, ensuring, regardless of cost, they get it. You sometimes have to read between the lines, of course, and sometimes consider your own needs in the process, but it's always worth making the effort and at times the sacrifice.

~ * ~

I popped my head through the brand new conservatory door and felt the warmth of the sunshine caress my face through the sparkling new glass. There was a gentle movement of refreshing air as the large fan turned silently above the small group lounging comfortably in the new suit of cane furniture. I gave them my broadest smile. "Good morning ladies," I chirped. "A wonderful Sunday morning. I hope we are all well?" There were consenting nods all round. "Back for lunch dear," I said, turning to my wife. I noted my smile was returned with interest.

As I closed the door gently behind me, the pleasant aroma of percolating coffee and freshly baked cakes lingered in my nostrils. I hesitated outside the door hearing my beloved again addressing her visitors.

"Yes, it is nice, isn't it," she cooed. "We did discuss having a summerhouse, you know. But the conservatory is so much more…" She hesitated, searching for the right word. "Well, so much more comfortable, don't you think? It somehow brings the garden *indoors*. A summerhouse would have been nice, of course, but so open to the elements. And when you really think about it, a summerhouse is little more than a fancy shed." I listened as, through mouthfuls of cake and sips of coffee, there came muffled murmurs of agreement.

I made my way contentedly to the front door. Mustn't hang around, George will have them in by now. He'll be wondering where on earth I've got to.

# FIXTURES AND FITTINGS

It was a sultry afternoon and he was glad it was his last call. He felt jaded; his crumpled, sweat stained shirt hot and sticky beneath his armpits. He turned into the lane, glancing at the clipboard on the seat beside him, confirming his instructions. Two hundred yards on the right, set back opposite open fields. She had warned him to be careful; it was on a bend and could easily be missed. He estimated the two hundred yards, slowed to a crawl and hoped nobody came up fast behind.

The rust-pitted, wrought iron sign indicating he had arrived at 'Three Views' hung lopsidedly on the gatepost, just visible through overhanging foliage. He turned carefully through the gate onto a concrete drive sandwiched between high, unchecked conifers and bush roses. It was five, maybe six cars long and, he thought, needed resurfacing, probably replacing. The garage at the end of the drive was a wooden structure and rotting badly. He stopped the car in front of the garage, reached for the clipboard and noted his initial thoughts.

Avoiding the rose thorns, he wriggled from the car and approached the front door. There was no response from several pushes at the doorbell so he rapped loudly on the door with his knuckles. He waited, stepping back and surveying the property, taking the opportunity to take the usual photographs. It was a typical 1960's bungalow in poor repair. Original wooden windows, also showing signs of rot, as was the front door. But, if the front garden was anything to go by, the bungalow sat on a large plot; that, at least, was a bonus.

With still no response to his knocking he again checked the clipboard. Yes, he had the right day. He pushed back the sleeve of his jacket and checked the time, noting with a little surprise he was almost fifteen minutes early. He hadn't realised, but it made a change; he was usually rushing to catch up. He would wait another fifteen minutes or so, but not in the car, it was too hot. The old garden bench sitting to one side of the front door looked inviting. It would be nice to relax in the shade for a few minutes. But he had barely sat down when he heard the front door scrape open.

She was elderly, withered and bent low. She leaned heavily on a stick, her free, claw-like hand clinging to the edge of the front door for additional support. Sparse, uncombed white hair lay like straw around her gaunt, hawkish features, sticking damply to one side of her face as if she had been sleeping. She wore a dark green blouse and heavy grey skirt covered by a pinafore. Her thin, bowed legs were sheathed in thick woollen stockings, her bony feet pushed awkwardly into fur-lined carpet slippers.

"Good morning," he called as he got to his feet and turned again toward the front door. "I'm from Edward's estate agents? Mrs Harper?"

At first she said nothing, just shuffled awkwardly backward, opening the door, motioning him in. When she did speak the words trembled faintly from thin, blue lips. "Sorry to keep you waiting," she said, pointing down the hall with the stick. Then, answering his question. "No, it's my daughter you want. She should be along shortly." She looked up at him with dull, rheumy eyes. "You're early, you know." Her words, he felt sure, were a reprimand.

She pushed the front door closed and beckoned him to follow as she shuffled slowly down the hall to a door at the far end. The hallway was dark; the musty smell familiar, typical of older unventilated properties. His eyes quickly took in his surroundings. The hall floor was covered in red linoleum with a single length of worn stair carpet running down its centre. Dark, heavily patterned wallpaper peeled down in several places from the ceiling. He hesitated for a second, missing little, writing quickly. The door at the far end of the hall led into a lounge. His eyes flicked round the room as he entered. It was, like the hall, old fashioned and obviously untouched for years. It happened as people got old, he thought; comfort found in things as they had always been, the urge to change, to keep up with the times diminishing with age. It was all too familiar. He afforded himself a little smile. Maybe he had been in the business too long; he had seen it all before. He found little to surprise him these days.

The old lady slumped gratefully into an armchair alongside an empty fireplace with long since spent ashes in the grate. Despite the heat of the day she dragged a blanket from the arm of the chair and draped it across her legs. Her face creased in a smile, paper thin, blue translucent skin drawn tight across her lips, her sharply protruding cheekbones threatening to break through.

She said nothing and for some moments he stood, unsure of what to do, feeling unusually uncomfortable and awkward.

"Don't let me stop you," she said finally. "You carry on. Just treat me as part of the furniture." Her smile broadened. "Just one of the fixtures and fittings, that's me, dear."

He nodded gratefully, backing toward the door. "Okay then, I'll get on with it, shall I"? She said nothing, but her dull eyes followed him disconcertingly from the room.

He had quickly found his way around the bungalow and before heading for the back garden, his last port of call, he had popped his head into the lounge. The old lady, the rug still drawn around her legs, was fast asleep. He quietly left her that way.

73

"Selling it at last, is she? The daughter?" The man, garden shears aloft, peered across the hedge. "Shouldn't leave a place empty for as long as that, you know."

He smiled. "No, I suppose not." His work was finished and remembering his own policy not to get involved with neighbours of potential sales, he edged toward the house.

"Sad case," the man persisted, following him along the hedge. "She loved the place, the old girl. The daughter tried to get her into a nursing home several times, but she wasn't having any of it. 'They'll never get me out, George, I'm here forever,' she told me, bless her. She wanted the daughter to come and live here, look after her, but there was no chance, not once she moved to London."

He edged closer toward the bungalow, the man in parallel, matching him step for step on the other side of the hedge. "Got a buyer yet, have you?"

He said nothing, just smiled and kept edging his way toward the door.

"Only seen the daughter once since the old girl died," the man persisted, still edging in unison. "She came up for the funeral. Said she was in no hurry to sell the place; might even rent it." He shook his head. "She's not worried; seems pretty well off, big car and all. But it shouldn't have been left this long, should it?"

He stopped edging, the man's words suddenly penetrating. "Sorry, you said the old girl. Who were you referring to?"

The man stumbled to a halt. "Pardon?"

"You said the old girl. Since the old girl died?"

"That's right. Old Mrs Harper, of course." He nodded toward the bungalow as if to emphasise his answer. "Spent almost half a century in the place, she did." He smiled, scratching his unshaven chin with the tip of the shears. "It won't be the same without her. But she was right; they

74

never did make her leave. Well, not until they carried her out, that is." He continued scratching absently. "Must be three months since. No one's been near or by, not even the daughter."

He frowned. "Well who..?" The words faltered on his lips, a cold trickle creeping between his shoulder blades.

"You all right, lad? You've turned quite pale. Probably the sun; shouldn't stay out in the sun too long, you know."

"I'm okay," he said, tucking the clipboard under his arm and quickly making his way back toward the bungalow. "Must be off."

"Hope you sell it soon," the man called after him. "Shouldn't be left empty too long, should it?"

They collided as he rounded the corner of the bungalow, his clipboard flying from his hand, clattering onto broken concrete. She was smartly dressed in a two-piece suit and though heavily made up, he guessed in her fifties.

"I'm terribly sorry," he said, recoiling against the wall.

"No, it was my fault," she replied breathlessly. "I was late; got snarled up in the traffic in town. I should have given myself more time. Shouldn't have been rushing. I always leave things to the last minute."

He stooped and retrieved the clipboard, noting as he straightened the gleaming BMW standing behind his own vehicle on the drive. "No harm done," he smiled, brushing concrete dust from his notes. "I'd just about finished anyway."

"Finished?"

"Yes." He held up the notes on the clipboard. "Got all I need; should be able to give a full valuation in a day or so."

"But don't you want to see inside?" She pulled a key from her pocket.

"Inside?"

"Yes. It won't be very impressive, I'm afraid; it's been shut up since mother died. I'm so busy, you see. But you really should look at the inside, shouldn't you?"

It was still very warm, the afternoon sun unrelenting. But somehow the stickiness beneath his armpits had chilled and the cold trickle between his shoulder blades refused to leave.

# WHY ME?

I read all about kidnapping. In fact I studied it in great detail. Innocent people, even the tiniest of children, stolen from their loved ones. Some never ever seeing the light of day again, others, some say the lucky ones, a ransom paid, returned to the bosom of their families. Then there were those like Terry Waite and John McCarthy; snatched from the street and held captive for years by political extremists.

Yes, I devoured all the books and watched all the TV programmes. I analyzed every word and studied each face as it told its story. Because, you see, I needed to be sure deep down, despite it all, despite being able to carry on with their lives, they really did feel the same. I needed to know it wasn't just me.

But as hard as I searched, as much as I studied others, I was never able to see it. I was never been able to detect the terrifying rage that forever boils within me, the utter hatred I have never been able to shed.

So now I know, the task ahead is mine and mine alone. Even as I sit and wait, knowing the day has finally come, the tortuous, never-ending replay continues to cascade through my mind.

The morning was like any other, the family chatting happily around the kitchen table. Then as always, father leaving, heading off to his business and leaving mother to do the school run. At the school gate it was the usual hug and kiss, embarrassing for a ten year old, but as an only child I was mother's whole world and any opportunity was keenly taken. Crossing the playground I turned for the final wave before entering the building and making for my classroom. A normal day, like any other.

It was mid morning when the school secretary poked her head around the classroom door. Mother had phoned; something she had forgotten to tell me. Nothing too important, but could I pop across to the school gate at break time?

Arriving at the gate I was surprised to find mother's car not there and at first took little notice of the other car and the man leaning casually against its side. But as I wandered out of the gate, looking from side to side, he pushed himself up and came toward me, a broad, friendly smile on his face.

"Hi Tim," he called. "Looking for your Mum?"

I nodded. "Yes, she asked me to meet her."

He laughed, a soft pleasant sound. "She had a bit of trouble. Her car broke down, so she asked if I would bring her here." He motioned toward the car.

They grind it into children from the earliest age, don't they? They never miss the opportunity. A mantra, over and over; never talk to strangers. Never ever talk to strangers. But at that moment, I was sure the face smiling from the back window of the car was my mother's. The man, his hand resting softly on my shoulder, gently guided me toward the car.

But the gentleness ended as soon as the car door was thrown open. Viciously gripped from behind, I was thrown forward across the back seat, my face ground savagely into the upholstery. I heard the door slam and the engine roar as the car jolted forward.

How long I was held there I don't know, but finally, gasping for air, I was released and allowed to sit up. But I was still held firmly by the woman sitting alongside me. Gripping my arm painfully, she yanked me toward her, pushing her face close to mine.

"Don't open your mouth, don't make a sound," she hissed, globules of spittle splattering my face. "You understand?"

Trembling uncontrollably, unable to comprehend, I stared, terrified, into the threatening eyes.

"*D'you understand*," she repeated, gripping my arm even harder.

Still unable to speak, I nodded.

I hardly dared move as the car sped on, the town eventually giving way to country roads surrounded by fields. After what seemed an eternity, the driver pulled into a narrow lane that led to a yard surrounded by barns. At the end of the yard stood an old farmhouse. The man and the woman dragged me from the car and pushed me roughly toward the house.

Inside I was led up the stairs and pushed through an open door into a tiny bedroom. The room was chilled and empty except for a small, metal-framed bed, its springs covered by a single mattress. The man closed the door behind us and instructed me to sit on the bed. Still shaking violently, I did as I was told.

He glared menacingly down at me with flint hard eyes. "Now you just listen to me," he said, his voice little more than a harsh whisper. "Do as you're told and nobody gets hurt, right?"

As I sat, alone and frightened, looking up at the threatening figures standing over me, the tears began to flow. "I want my Mum," I sobbed.

He took a step toward me, bent forward and slapped me hard across the face. The force of the blow knocked me back across the bed, my head colliding painfully with the wall. The shock of the vicious blow instantly stopped me crying. I lay on the bed, my hand held to my stinging cheek, staring petrified at the two expressionless faces looking down at me.

"That's better," the man said. He grinned menacingly. "We don't want no silly blubbing, do we?"

He pulled some thick cord from his pocket and between them they tied my hands and feet, finally securing my bound hands to the metal bed rail.

"He's not going anywhere fast, is he?" The man laughed. It was a deep coarse sound that still torments my dreams.

Finally the woman sealed my mouth with wide sticky tape. The man nodded, satisfied, and they turned to leave. "I'll get you some grub," he said as he pulled open the door. "Then we'll get down to business."

A little later they came back into the room, the woman carrying a plate with a sandwich and a steaming mug.

They untied my hands and peeled the tape from my mouth. Pulling me round, they sat me on the edge of the bed.

"Now eat and we'll tell you what you've got to do," the man said.

Terrified, I nibbled at the sandwich and sipped tentatively at the unpleasantly strong tea, conscious of the watching eyes. Soon, becoming impatient, the woman sat on the bed alongside me. She produced a small recording machine which she held in front of my face.

"All you have to do is say what I tell you, right?"

Still clasping the half eaten sandwich and the mug in my trembling hands, I nodded obediently.

It took several attempts, my quivering lips struggling to form cohesive words, but eventually I spoke into the machine. The message was aimed at my mother and was a simple instruction. I was safe for now, but to keep it that way she had to do as the man told her. Satisfied, they re-tied my hands, put more tape across my mouth and left me alone.

Much later I learned the message, played over a mobile phone, was accompanied by a demand for a great deal of money. Pay up and the boy survives. Refuse and you'll never see him again.

It was dark when the man returned to the room, but he didn't bother to turn on the light. His large, threatening shadow stood outlined by the landing light behind, his face a black mass. He told me he had

80

spoken to my parents and if I was a very good boy, I would be seeing them again very soon. He again pulled the tape from my mouth but warned if I made a single sound, I would never see anyone ever again. He drew his finger across his throat to emphasize the threat. Then I was left alone in the chilled, frightening blackness. Petrified he would hear, I stifled my endless sobs into the mattress.

They played my parents for two months; eight terrifying weeks, during which time I was only released from my bonds to eat and to use the toilet. Then one day they burst into the room, quickly released my bonds and rushed me down the stairs and out into the car. They drove for some time before stopping on an isolated country road and pushing me out.

My father was a wealthy man, but to be able to pay the ransom, he'd used all his resources and more. Some would say as a result I was one of the lucky ones. But maybe those people wouldn't understand what eight weeks of constant terror could do to a ten year old. They may also not have experienced what it is like to be reunited with a mother whose brain had been turned by those same eight tormenting weeks. A mother who henceforth needed constant medication to maintain anything like a rational head and whose paranoid antics eventually caused an irreversible split with her financially ruined husband. No, they may not appreciate any of that.

Maybe every case is different. Maybe some can return and in time pick up from where they left off. Maybe they really can. And if I am the odd one out, the only one that needs more, needs closure, then so be it.

My father's money has never been recovered and only the man was ever caught. It was almost a year later when, from behind a screen, I was able to confirm the identification the police were seeking. The man was convicted and sentenced, some said harshly. But he didn't get a life sentence. Not like my mother, who never recovered and now needs constant supervision. Nor like my father, who was never able to retrieve his ruined business and died a broken man. And not like me; tormented ever since by the constant fear and terrible hatred embedded within me. No, not like any of us. Time passes. Sentences, however long, come to an end.

But I have been patient. I've waited.

I still ask myself, why me? Why only me? But as I watch, my eyes unable to leave the prison gate, the alien, cold steel of the pistol butt clasped in my jacket pocket, I know the time for questions is over. Whatever the consequences, it is now time for closure.

# WHAT THE EYE DON'T SEE

Leaving the cottage, he quietly closed the door and lowered the latch gently behind him. For several minutes he stood motionless, staring into the night sky, pupils dilating, absorbing every tiny precious particle of available light, his whole being relishing the moonless darkness as it settled around him like a comforting, silken cloak. He breathed slowly, deeply, filling his lungs, savouring the soft night air. When finally he moved, his progress was slow and measured, his footfalls catlike. He padded down the path and through the ageing gate, its rusting hinges the only protesting sound in the silent blackness. Within seconds he had melted into the outer fringes of the forest.

Night-time and the forest. This was his time, his world. This was where light was an unnecessary intrusion. This was where he came alive, where every muscle, every fibre of his being strained with blood-rushing intensity. It was where he wanted to be, always.

He hoisted the large canvas bag into a comfortable position on his shoulder and moved confidently forward. It would be a long night, there were many snares to check, much to do, but that was the pleasure of it all.

As he made his way silently through the undergrowth, thoughts of his childhood, his early initiation, returned. He smiled affectionately at the memory. At first the long days roaming the forest with his father. Back and forth, twisting this way and that, learning, memorizing.

Then there were the nights.

No more than a child, terrified in the utter blackness, dogging his father's footsteps and clinging to the short piece of cord; the only thing averting separation and a path to oblivion. And his father's whispered instructions, always the whispers. Even now, so many years later, his father long since departed, he could still hear the whispers.

"You don't need the light, boy. Anyone can see in the light. Just remember what you've seen before and draw the mental map. Move slowly and be sure. Use your ears, measure your steps and feel for the markers, they'll tell you that you're right; they'll confirm the map. Make the night your friend, boy, and it will always give up its riches."

In time the cord had been discarded, the physical link broken. He had been cast adrift in the frightening blackness. But the whispers remained and gradually, as his father had promised it would, the map formed in his head. Soon he too had set his markers and the frightening darkness had slowly become a comforting friend.

He stopped and reached forward. His fingertips, as he knew they would, touched the rough bark of a four hundred year old oak: his marker, the confirmation of the map. He thought again of how, even now, so long after his passing, he still missed his father: consummate woodsman, mentor and most of all, best friend.

Oh, and yes, and utter rogue who, in the tradition of generations of his ancestors, capitalized on the briefest of opportunities.

And like those generations before him, father was tolerated, accepted as an essential part of the local economy. But only under the premise that what the eye didn't see, the heart would never grieve. Therefore, as it had forever been, night-time and its darkness were the crucial ingredients of their trade.

But times had changed and things were different now. There was still an outlet for his merchandise, but it was small and ever dwindling. A tradition of generations was dying and the time for change was upon him.

But it was all he knew, it was all his family had ever known. It wasn't the darkness that frightened him now, it was the future. He sighed sadly and moved on, deeper into the woods.

It was later when resting his back against a towering elm, the usual chocolate bar and warm coffee for sustenance, when he first heard it, an alien sound. Not the usual, recognizable cough of a muntjac deer or the yak of a fox, but more...

He sat perfectly still, the chocolate bar an inch from his lips, remembering. "Use your ears before you move." His beloved father's whispers always hovering.

Then, there it was again. He frowned in the darkness, his mind calculating, judging the direction, the distance, deeper in the forest. It was the early hours and nothing ever moved so deep in the forest at this hour. Nothing human, that was. And this was human, of that he was sure.

He finished the chocolate bar, important energy, and stowed the tiny coffee flask before moving on. His movements were even more cautious now; he was detouring away from his normal route, away from the map, his brain recalculating a new, virtual plot, his ears drawing him ever closer to the sound.

The light, when he first saw it, was just a flicker, a momentary flash then gone. A torch, he thought, someone moving around. His progress slowed as he edged from marker to marker, finally sinking to his haunches among the brush, his quarry now in full sight.

He knew where he was, knew his exact position. The narrow track he was looking down upon was the one single thoroughfare through the northern end of the forest. It was little known and rarely used even in the daytime. And yet, here, in the early hours, stood the 4x4; the sound of its engine softly ticking over, the muted grunts of the two individuals struggling with two large sacks at its side.

He watched as, by the light of the single torch, the two men manhandled the sacks into a thicket well away from the track. Then a different sound; the sound of digging. Leaving his position, he made his way carefully down to the 4x4. He was there for just a few moments before once again sliding silently back into the undergrowth. There he waited patiently.

~ * ~

His sleep was deep and untroubled and it was some moments before the pounding on the cottage door brought him to full consciousness. He eased himself out of the bed and pulled on his trousers, slipping the braces over his shoulders. Pushing his feet into the slippers at the side of the bed, he made his way, bleary eyed, down the narrow stairs to the front door. Of the two men standing on the doorstep, he knew one. The village bobby introduced the second man as a Detective Inspector from the city CID.

"Mind if we come in for a chat?" the inspector asked.

He shook his head and led them down the narrow passage and into the tiny sitting room.

"The Inspector has a problem," the local bobby started. "I told him it was doubtful anyone could help then I thought of you. Told him the only chance might be you."

The Inspector nodded. "The constable tells me nobody knows the forest around here like you."

He scratched at his unshaven chin and shrugged. "Could be so."

"He says you know just about everything that goes on in there."

He smiled. "'Tis a big forest, that's for sure. Can't know everything."

"Were you in the forest last night?"

"Last night? Can't say I was."

The Inspector eyed him thoughtfully for a moment. "Look," he said finally, "I'm not suggesting you were in the forest last night, but if you were you can relax. I'm not interested in what you were doing there. I just need your help. Do you understand what I'm saying?"

He frowned and shook his head. "Can't say I do."

The Inspector sighed, but persevered. "Look, yesterday morning two men carried out a robbery in the city. They got away with a very substantial sum of money. The money, all used notes, would have taken quite a bit of shifting; it filled two large sacks."

"That's a lot of money," he said, shaking his head.

"Yes, a great deal of money. But, in the early hours of this morning, the police received a telephone call. The caller, a man, told of two individuals seen burying something in the forest. More than that, he gave the exact location of where the stuff was buried and the registration number of the vehicle they were using."

"You got the call in the early hours?"

The Inspector nodded. "Yes, at 2.17am exactly."

He frowned. "You mean someone, other than those with the money, I mean, was in the forest at that time?"

Again the Inspector nodded. "Yes, they must have been."

"Strange that," he said thoughtfully. "No moon last night. You'd 'ave to be able to see in the dark to be in the forest at such a time? Wonder who would want to do that?"

Puffing out his cheeks, the local constable turned and looked out of the window.

"We don't know because he refused to give us his name," the Inspector said. "But we do know the call was made from the public telephone box, here in the village. We can only think, a local man."

He shook his head. "Mystery to me."

The muscles along the Inspector's jaw tightened. "Well, I have two mysteries," he said, an irksome edge creeping into his voice. "This morning we picked up the two men who carried out the robbery and we retrieved the money."

He smiled. "Pleased with that, I bet. But that's no mystery, is it?"

"No, the mystery is the money we got back was somewhat less than was stolen."

"You mean the robbers had already spent some?"

The Inspector sighed. "At that time in the morning? I somehow doubt it."

He shrugged. "You said two mysteries."

The Inspector, at last giving up, turned toward the door. "The other mystery is close by to where we dug up the sacks we found several dead rabbits. Looked to us as if someone had disposed of them. Maybe emptied a bag." He turned and looked back with icy, accusing eyes. "Now why would anyone do that, d'you think?"

He shook his head. "Now that I wouldn't know," he said, holding the Inspector's stare, unflinching, innocent. "But dead rabbits? All I can say is myxomatosis has been bad this year."

He heard the front door close behind his visitors and from the window watched them move down the path to the waiting police car.

"Make the night your friend, boy, and it will always give up its riches." He couldn't be sure, but he thought this time he detected a proud chuckle in the whisper running through his head. Maybe it was telling him something. Maybe it was saying there was no need to be frightened of the future, that one way or the other the night would always provide for him.

# IDENTITY

I couldn't be sure which it was that had dragged me from my unconscious state; the foul tasting fur in my mouth was in itself bad enough, but the blinding pain in my right eye was something I had not previously encountered. And though I have to admit, of late, neither the morning after sewer like tang or the brain-loosening headache were strangers, a skewer being driven into my eyeball was disturbing.

I made to roll onto my back then my side, any position other than that which welded me to the bed at present. It was a precarious move. Apart from muscles, which appeared immovably seized, indicating at least a stroke, there was the bladder to consider. Full to overflowing, the slightest pressure in the wrong place could cause a disaster.

So, movement of the body would take further consideration. I was, however, able to move my head and by doing so, to my great relief, the pain in my eye began to recede. And by forcing my gunk glued eyelids apart and blinking them into some sort of semi-blurred focus, I realized why. A thin slither of extraordinarily bright sunlight had forced its way between the only chink in my otherwise tightly drawn curtains. It had focused the full force of its attention on the only part of my person visible above the duvet, my right eye. So it was confirmed. I hadn't had a stroke and as far as I could see at this early stage, my vision was unimpaired.

Time to get up then. But to get up in the morning, especially at the weekend, you have to have a reason and I couldn't think of a single one. It was therefore much later, having been given a final ultimatum by my bladder, I found myself perched on the edge of the bed.

The bedroom, like the rest of the flat, was a mess. I knew it and I didn't care. You see, like getting out of bed, you have to have a reason for keeping the place clean and tidy. Also like getting out of bed--notwithstanding the bladder thing, of course--I didn't have one. And before I hear you cry lazy slob, you should be aware it hasn't always been this way. There was a time when everything was spick and span--well as spick and span as any healthy, single young male could make it. But that was when what seemed like a lifetime of classrooms and exams had ended and life, real life, had begun. It was also when there was ambition and optimism. More, it was when there was a rampant enthusiasm.

You see, it had never been just a wish, never just a desire. It had always been nothing less than a burning obsession. From that very first day at nursery school when a piece of wallpaper had been laid, face down, in front of me. When a crayon had been thrust into my tiny paw. When I drew that first line. And it wasn't colours or drawing pictures that interested me. No, it was the shape, the form and most of all the identity of what appeared as I ran that crayon across the wallpaper's bumpy rear surface. As I progressed, those lines gave up their identity in the form of what I saw then and have seen ever since as the most fascinating of all things: words.

Writing became my life, all I ever wanted to do. I was destined to be an author. And not just any old author. I was to be a famous, blockbuster of an author. People from all over the world would flock to read my work. There would be endless queues outside bookshops. Harry Potter would fade into insignificant history.

I shuffled to the bathroom and afterwards, relieved, moved zombie-like to the kitchen and the kettle. The cheap whiskey bottle stood on the table.

Empty.

I tried to remember when I had bought it; worse, when I had drunk it. I gave up.

As I waited for the kettle I recalled how well it had started. A well paid job had ensured I wanted for little. And I had tried, I really had. But I knew it was just a substitute, a stopgap until those multinational publishers started to clamour for my work. I found it difficult to concentrate, my mind always elsewhere. Plots were constantly forming, characters forcing themselves to the fore, demanding to be recognised. Workmates were characterized as heroes and villains, all intertwined in complicated scenarios.

The kettle boiled and I shovelled coffee into a mug and stirred it to a black mass. I was at the door before I remembered. The whiskey; just a splash. The hair of the dog. I turned and again looked at the empty bottle. Damn. I slumped into a chair. Another pointless weekend had begun.

As he ranted at me, I remember looking past him, through the glass door into the outer office. The grinning faces. They knew. They all knew. The Walter Mitty of the office; I'd heard them talk. His angry words continued. It wasn't good enough. I was supposed to secure contracts, not make stupid schoolboy mistakes and loose them.

Fair cop, guv. There was little I could say to defend myself. And anyway, there was little I wanted to say. I just stood and studied his raving, considering the dialogue, slotting him into character-second arch villain, nasty but not very intelligent, vocabulary most certainly lacking. Only the last few words broke through.

"Such tardiness could not be tolerated. We will have to let you go."

Cradling the coffee, my knees drawn up, I surveyed the room. When I had taken the flat, I'd had visions. This is where it would all start. The workstation in the corner strategically positioned alongside the window so I could scan the outside world as I sought inspiration. The specially selected laptop, the dictionaries, thesaurus, fact finders, all in place. It would go down in history as the place where genius had been spawned. I had started with such gusto, the words flying onto the screen. Wonderful words become sentences, sentences paragraphs. Chapter after chapter until finally it was done. It was time to for the world to sample the first of the wonders to come.

But over time something had been lost and the tiny room no longer engendered the enthusiasm it once had. My eyes wandered from the workstation to the wall above. Don't worry, they said. Everybody gets 'em, they said. Even the best. Don't be despondent. Paper the walls with them and later, when you are famous, you will smile and say to those struggling to emulate you, "I know how you feel. I've been there."

And I had done just that. I had pasted the first rejection slip above the screen, directly in front of my eyes. And I had smiled. But then one had become two, two had become three and three...

It had taken time to recover from the humiliation of the dismissal. But it had made me think. Despite my qualifications, a responsible job was not what was required. Anything would do provided it paid the bills. And that was how it was. I looked down at my hands, callused from the manual tasks that for five days each week were now my daily routine. Just a stopgap I had told myself. Just for a short time until those publishers recognise the mistake they had made.

So, the weekend was here. Up and at 'em, boy, the keyboard awaits. The publishers are still there. Nothing has changed. I sighed and looked again at the wall above the workstation. No, nothing had changed. I made for the kitchen. Maybe another coffee, something to kick-start the day.

I was vaguely aware of the sound of mail dropping through the letterbox, but ignored it. The most recent rejection slip had arrived several days before. I had nothing else out there, nothing to look forward to.

I made the coffee, just as black as the first. Nursing the mug, I wandered to the front door and picked up the magazine, my writing magazine, that lay on the doormat.

More advice, more tips. How to get published? Yeah, right.

Back in the chair I flicked through the pages. I'd seen it all before, even participated. The short story competition-at least you didn't receive a rejection slip for failing at that.

But hang on. The words; the shape, the form, the identity. *My identity.* It stood out bold and proud. There was no mistake. I had been short-listed. Think about that, my son. People from far and wide, across the world, had tried and of them all I had been short-listed.

Back in the kitchen, the coffee found its way down the sink. I moved from room to room, throwing back the curtains, letting the bright sunlight flood in. Now what? A shave, a shower, that's it. Then I must get this placed cleaned up. Can't work in a pig's sty, can I?

In the lounge I waved the magazine at the rejection slip covered wall and laughed.

"It's your loss, guys," I crowed. "Cause you ain't seen nothin' yet.

# I ALWAYS GOT AWAY WITH IT

"I always get away with it."

Someone was turning a corkscrew in his stomach.

"Every time?"

"Every time."

"So it never fails?"

"Never has yet." His mouth was tinder dry and the blood drummed in his temples.

He let the silence hang, watching the man sitting opposite twist the long since empty coffee cup nervously between his fingers, at one with the turmoil surging through him. But the man's expression, the excited gleam in his eyes gave it all away. He was on the very verge of going for it.

They both knew they were playing a dangerous game. The stakes were tremendously high and caution, extreme caution was paramount if they were to pull it off. If just one whiff of this conversation got into the wrong hands, the whole world would come crashing down around them both. They would be finished.

And for the man facing him, that was only a fraction of the concern. There were those behind him, his backers, those of supposedly high repute. They too knew the fearful risks. Lives could be ruined, reputations shredded. But in the perilous, knife edged world in which

94

they all lived the competition was intense and for those who were just one step ahead the rewards were huge. Those waiting on his decision were willing to walk the tightrope, but only if they could be sure, absolutely certain of success. And they looked to him for that success. Failure was not an option.

That was why they were closeted in the tiny motel room, its curtains drawn, their voices lowered to unnecessary whispers. Just the two of them. That was why he felt breathless, why the blood zinged in his veins and beads of sweat clung to his upper lip. He had embarked upon the most perilous path and though, unlike the man opposite, he had no one but himself to worry about, the risks were still huge. But it was the only way. He was under no illusion, without this he was destined for oblivion.

Fame is a double-edged curse. With it comes a blood pounding exhilaration, a wondrous awe at being the centre of attraction, at the incessant demand to be seen and heard. But with it, in time, also comes the realisation there is the constant, bone aching pressure to maintain those exacting standards the adoration demands. And that however good you are at what you do, is never possible. And when, despite your every effort, those standards begin to slip, there comes the overwhelming desire to hide away, to scramble into a corner, a hole, anywhere to escape the attention. But you can't, because by then you are hooked; you need the attention like an addict needs a fix. If fame does begin to slip away, if the adulation does wane, moves to the new kid on the block, then your world crumbles.

And his world had crumbled. He knew he no longer had what it took. He knew however hard he tried, he could no longer be what he had once been. And now he knew those who still looked to him for their continued success knew it also. His time was almost up. They had been nice about it, of course, but he had to understand their position. Success was all that mattered and despite any technological advantages they might

95

have, success was not happening. He had tried to explain. It was just a blip; he was going through a bad patch. Everybody had them, didn't they? But it was no good. They couldn't afford to wait. They needed the success now. It was all that mattered.

The adoration and the lifestyle it brought with it would all too soon come to an end. Before, the future, the end he knew had to come, had been but a distant horizon. Now it was here, on his doorstep. He had to make provision for it in any way he could. Pull this off and though life would never be the same, he would at least be financially secure. He should have been anyway, of course, but his past ultra lavish lifestyle and more, his rash, ill advised and wayward investments had sucked him dry. Now he was left with this one hope.

"When can you get the details?" The other man's voice was little more than a brittle, hoarse whisper. He had made the decision.

It hadn't been a lie. Never, in the hundreds of times he had tried it, had it let him down. And at the moment it was available only to him. But it was only a small part. An imperative part, but still only a part of what was needed to achieve complete success. The rest was down to him and it was the rest he no longer had. All too soon his rule would be over; his last race would have been run. Then the opportunity would be lost. It was now or never.

He had chosen them carefully knowing they were struggling the most. They were constantly probing, searching for something, anything that would bring them up to par with the opposition. Maybe even give them the edge. His first approach had been tentative and purposely phrased as a joke. Their reaction had been as he had hoped, but equally as cautious. He knew then they had taken the bait. The die had been cast.

Getting the basic information was simple. He was there, he was part of the team, there were no secrets. It was the printed data that would prove a little more difficult. Without it there would be no deal. But to be able to carry out his job, to be able to get the very best out of the equipment, it was necessary for him to know that technical detail, to understand how everything worked. The chance came, as he knew it would, at a full design briefing. The camera was tiny and designed particularly for macro photography. He'd had just those few moments alone, the one single opportunity, but it was enough. He should have felt guilty; it was a betrayal of trust. But he didn't. They had cast him aside without a second thought. He owed them nothing.

It was China and the last race of the season. It was also the last race of his career. Someone else will have you, they had said. One of the lesser teams desperate for experience. Then, a season, maybe two, and who knows, maybe the old brilliance, the old daring would return. The world would be his oyster again. But that was not to be. All the seats had been taken; fearless, death defying young guns. Nobody had wanted a fading star.

As he climbed into the cramped compartment, wriggling into the familiar position for the last time, he knew there would be no reason to perform. Even a win, which was little short of impossible, would do nothing more than boost his own ego. So why should he? Take your time, he told himself. A two hour cruise, safe and secure, no need to rush. The deed had been done, the money was in the bank, now was not the time to take risks.

Through his visor he studied the rear of the car in front, a wry smile touching his lips clamped securely within the padding of the helmet. Strange how they should have qualified in that position, directly in front of him. They had moved quickly, the new design already installed in the car, their initial tests so successful they were already using it in anger in this, the last race of the season. It would give them the winter to improve or carry out minor adjustments. It had all gone so smoothly. No one had suspected. Eyebrows would be raised today.

The red lights seemed to hang for an eternity before extinguishing, the roar of twenty-two super charged engines screaming to a crescendo around him. He dropped the clutch and floored the accelerator, feeling the gloriously phenomenal power as the car surged forward, knowing instantly this would not be a cruise. No, this time he would show them. This time they would know they had made the wrong decision. This would be the drive of his life.

But in the split second it took to thrust his right foot to the floor, the single movement sending the car hurtling eagerly, faultlessly, forward, he realised this was not to be the drive of his life. It was not to be a drive at all. Instead he saw the rear of the car in front grinding toward him, eating the fragile front of his magnificent machine, chewing its way toward him.

It could not be. It was not possible. His very last race, the only chance left to prove they were all wrong; that the skill, the daring was still there, that he did still have what it took. But no, not today, not now, not ever again.

But how? It was impossible. Hadn't he given them the plans? And hadn't they told him? It was installed, proven. This would be the race. How was it possible the stupid driver hadn't got away? How was it with the most sophisticated clutch and gearbox system ever designed, the car had stalled in front of him? He felt the searing pain as his own car drove inexorably forward, the rear of the stationary vehicle in front grinding into his feet his ankles his knees. Entombed in the helmet, his unbelieving, screamed words were drowned by the deafening roar of the other cars around him.

"But I always got away with it."

# CLOSE TO THE DARK SIDE

Hands clasped behind him, shoulders pulled back, the Chief Superintendent drew himself up to his full height, which I thought cynically, probably only just made the regulation minimum.

"Well now, what can I say about Inspector George Rawlings?"

I watched him from the corner of my eye, standing alongside me, a malicious grin touching the corners of his mouth. "No, let me re-phrase that. What can I say that's good about Inspector George Rawlings?" The grin widened and a ripple of embarrassed laughter circulated the room.

I felt my skin creep. It was bad enough the dreaded day had arrived. No need to milk it. Why didn't the pompous prat just get it over with? Thanks a bunch, now on your bike. That would do and it was what he wanted to say anyway. But no, there was history, lots of it, and he would savour the moment. And worse, I had to stand and bear it, even smile at the snide cracks that were sure to come. My final day and my old enemy, my boss and the last person I wanted beside me at this time, would have the last laugh. Well, maybe. Then again maybe not.

We had joined at the same time, more than thirty years before, but had taken very different paths. Him the political route; seeking the headlines, never straying from the course of correctness, adhering to every rule and clinging only to those who could benefit him and his career. Me a loner who loved life in the gutter of crime. A street copper whose whole world revolved around the continuous grind of piecing together the jigsaw that finally led to an arrest. And promotion? No big deal. If it came, it came.

I had heard much about him over the years--you only had to read the newspapers for that--but our paths had only converged when eighteen months before, as our new Chief Superintendent, he had descended on the nick with a fanaticism for the regulations, for tidiness and order and in particular for scrupulously written reports that had shaken the whole team. The confrontations between us had started instantly, becoming more vitriolic as time passed. They had continued to this, my last day.

And the reason? As far as I was concerned the rules were made for bending, and reports, which did little more than supply the hierarchy with fuel to fire their own glory hunting, were a waste of precious policing time. No, solve the crime, catch the criminal and move on. It was what we were here for. No time for pen pushing, no time for praise or stardom. I was a front line copper; it was my job. More, it was my life. Some said I was so close to the dark side had I not been a copper I would have been a master criminal. Now there's a thought.

"No, no, I'm joking of course," he went on, the smile dropping dramatically from his face. "There is an awful lot that can be said about George here." He rested his hand awkwardly on my shoulder. It was the first time he had physically touched me and it didn't feel comfortable. I smiled dutifully, resisting an overwhelming temptation to pull away.

"But first of all, let me congratulate George for being able to maintain his lifetime devotion to bachelorhood." Cat calls from the back of the room and the Super' nodded. "Yes, there will be those who envy him that freedom. Though I have to say, and I'm sure George will forgive me for this, there are times when a woman's touch wouldn't go amiss."

I maintained the tight-lipped smile. The first attack about my appearance had come within days of his arrival at the nick. To no avail it had continued ever since. Even on my last day, he couldn't let go. No, he was wrong. I wouldn't forgive him.

Realizing he was to get no response he moved on. "George and I go back a long way. We joined the force together and though we went our separate ways a long time ago, I tried to maintain contact."

Lying git. When he'd arrived at the nick I'd had to remind him we had known each other previously.

"Yes, I do feel I can speak with some authority about George's career." The hand remained on the shoulder. "There are some that would say with more than thirty years under his belt he should have made more than a mere Inspector."

Yup, I was expecting that one. The camouflaged reminder he had made the heady heights, scaled the ladder, and I had bounced along the bottom rung.

Bastard.

"But let that not be said, because where would we be without the likes of George, those who are happy to be the foot soldiers of our great institution?"

*Foot soldier?* **Foot soldier?** *Now that's nasty. Don't forget, you rat bag, I'm an Inspector. And maybe, if it weren't for you and your... No, don't let's go there.*

"And there are those who would be only too pleased to remind George that his greatest case, despite his best efforts, was also his greatest failure."

The room fell silent and all eyes turned toward me. Even I was stunned. I had expected the underhanded digs, it was his last chance and I knew they would come. But not this. He had broken the rule. On the one day when old animosities should be put to one side; when despite the past all cracks should be papered over, he had chosen to drive the final nail. Even for him, it was way below the belt. Looking straight ahead I said nothing, just shrugged my shoulders. He felt the chill. He had gone too far and he knew it.

"I mention this only in praise," he went on quickly, too quickly, too late. "Because those who live in glass houses should never cast the first stone. We've all had our failures, most hidden within the immense workload we undertake. It just happened to be George's incredible bad luck to front a major crime investigation involving the loss of millions. A crime so audacious it created media frenzy that lasted for months. A policeman's nightmare. Only his dogged determination and professionalism saw him through that dark time and I commend him for that. We must each ask ourselves, what if it had been any one of us? Could we have handled ourselves with such dignity?"

A bitter bile rose to the back of my throat. *But it hadn't been you, had it? It had been me, you bastard. And why was it me? Because you had scuttled into the shadows and hung me out to dry, that's why. Because you, always ready to step into the limelight, to front the press interviews when things went well, had recognised the danger signs and backed away from what was an inevitable disaster. I, too, had seen the light, seen that those involved were too big, too powerful for us ever to bring to justice. But there was nowhere for me to hide, was there? I had to stand and take it.* I gulped at the glass of beer I had almost forgotten I was holding, easing the bitterness at the back of my throat.

"So, George, what does retirement hold for you?" He had overstepped the mark. Now he wanted to get it over with, get out quickly.

I retained the smile. "I'm going to live abroad."

"Abroad?" He smiled, casting his eyes round the room. "Not Spain, I hope. Not joining our old adversaries on the Costa del crime."

"No nothing like that. I have property in Miami." More catcalls and cheers from around the room.

A frown creased his brow. "Miami, Florida?"

"Yes, on the coast. A large waterside property, a boat, plenty of sunshine, you know the sort of thing. Think I deserve it, don't you?"

His mouth fell open. He was an arrogant prig. A jumped up, conceited prat who had achieved his position by sucking up to those that could do him the most good and disappearing when the shit hit the fan. But he was a copper; he had trained like the rest of us and as I held his gaze I could see the results of that training coming into play. Slowly but surely he was making the connections as I'd hoped he would. He had known as well as I who had been involved, how the vast sums of money had disappeared. He had also known where it had gone. But the perpetrators were too hot to handle; lofty individuals who at the slightest hint of exposure could destroy reputations and ruin careers with a single telephone call. Now, if you are someone whose life has been dedicated to building a career, well what do you do?

But let's say you are a lowly inspector, a bachelor whose whole existence had been his job. And let's say you were fast approaching retirement and because of that devotion to the job you had made little or no preparation for retirement. And let's also say, after considering all that, you are a gutter cop who it's been said has always been just a whisker away from the other side, the dark side. No reputation, no career, nothing to lose. Well, to some, your silence could be worth a fortune, couldn't it?

# RESPECT

An early summer sun sat just above the horizon, the morning already warming to its rays, as the old man picked his way carefully down the ancient wooden steps to the beach. Easing himself from the last time worn tread he stood for some moments, absently wriggling his aching, arthritic toes in the soft, white sand, his rheumy eyes traversing the ocean before him. Only tiny ripples gently caressed the shoreline, but despite this, the old man could sense a tension in the vast expanse.

If asked, he could not have explained it, other than a sixth sense, an awareness born of a lifetime spent in tiny boats, getting to know this huge mistress who day after day tolerated men like himself, grudgingly supplying them with their livelihood. Sometimes it was a meager livelihood, for she never relinquished her riches readily, but it was a livelihood nonetheless. And if you were lucky, if you quickly learned to read the signs, to judge her moods and respect her wishes, then you survived. If not...

The old man made his way slowly along the beach toward the gaggle of boats pulled haphazardly up on the soft white sand.

"No later than noon today," he muttered to himself. "The old girl will want us out of her hair by lunchtime today."

A group of young men stood talking, from time to time their raucous laughter drifting across to the old man's ears.

"Good morning, old man," one of them called as he approached. "How are you today? Ready for the catch of your life?" The greeting sounded friendly, but the old man could detect the usual mocking tone, see the conspiratorial grins on the faces of the others. He said nothing, just nodded a greeting as he did every morning and turned his attention to his tiny boat, conscious of their eyes upon him as he pulled off the worn tarpaulin cover and folded it meticulously, stowing it in the stern.

He didn't blame them. It was not their fault. They were the product of the modern world, a world that promoted a younger generation to believe only they mattered. The old man, he knew, represented a forgotten time no longer of any consequence. How could they be expected to see him as anything other than a relic from a past age?

It was different in his youth when the older generation had commanded respect; when their years had given them the vast experience and knowledge the young could only hope, in time, to attain. But now that respect had been replaced by, at best total disregard, at worst derision. He sighed sadly as he moved around his little boat checking that the ancient outboard motor was secure, that there was plenty of fuel and the oars, though these days a precaution only, were secured in the bottom of the boat.

Satisfied, the old man relaxed against the side of his little boat. He pulled a short-stemmed pipe from his pocket, its bowl black and disfigured by many years of smoldering daily use, and casually filled it from a brown stained, plastic pouch. Tamping the tobacco tightly in the bowl, he clamped the pipe, unlit, between his teeth and moved to the back of the little boat. It was time to go.

As his father had taught him a lifetime before, the old man buried his feet into the sand and leaned his back against the stern of the little boat. And as he knew it would, as it always did, the little boat at first refused to move. Again he was conscious of the eyes of the young men upon him. Did they think today the little boat would beat him, would refuse to budge? Were they hoping this would be the day he would need to ask for help? The pale lips formed a thin, satisfied smile around the pipe as the old man applied the extra pressure he knew to be needed. The little boat finally broke free from the sand's grip, slowly gathering momentum and slithering eagerly to the water's edge.

The old man continued to push, wading himself into the water, until the little craft lifted from the sand and bobbed happily in the shallows. He eased the ancient outboard's propeller into the water and hoisted himself aboard. A single pull was all that was needed and the little engine spluttered into life. The old man held a match to the short-stemmed pipe clamped between his teeth, drawing hard until the tobacco glowed, then turning the tiller, he opened the throttle and his little boat headed out to sea.

He had emptied the majority of his pots and set fresh by just after eleven. His catch was as good as any he'd had recently. The fishmongers would be pleased and he would eat well tonight. He debated continuing; completing his trawl, but sniffing the lessening breeze and noting the ever-increasing swell, he knew he was no longer welcome out here. She was telling him it was time to go and as always he would respect her wishes.

Earlier, as he had gently made his way out to his pots, two of the young men in their bigger, more powerful boat, its huge outboard foaming in its wake, had overtaken him. They had passed the old man's little boat, laughing as their powerful bow wave had pitched it from one side to the other. With their larger vessel they were heading further out, making for deeper water. Now as the old man turned his little boat toward the shore, he looked back, out toward that deeper water. The heavy swell rose and fell ever larger and a mist descended, rapidly following him shoreward.

"Yes," he muttered to himself. "She wants us out of her hair before lunchtime, that's for sure."

But as the old man headed toward the shore, a feeling of apprehension began to envelope him, a foreboding he could not explain, even understand. Again he looked seaward, straining his eyes and ears. But he could see nothing, hear nothing, the thickening mist deadening both sound and vision. For some minutes he held his course, knowing the worsening conditions demanded he make it to shore and safety as soon as he could, remembering his father's words. "She will always let you know when it's time to go, lad, when she no longer wants you pillaging her larder. Always heed her, never ignore her warnings."

The words had stayed with the old man always, forever imprinted on his memory. As were the events of the day when his father, so wise, so experienced, had himself ignored her warning. The day when the catch had been so good he had stayed, unable to resist.

The one day in his whole life he had not heeded his own warning, not respected her wishes. And his father had paid the ultimate price for that one moment of disrespect.

But despite this, despite not even knowing why he was making such a perilous decision, the old man found himself moving the tiller, the tiny little boat turning, again heading seaward.

As the old man steered the tiny boat further out, away from the shore and safety, the mist thickened and the air chilled around him. His eyes probed the gloom before him, occasionally flicking skyward, calculating the time of day, desperately seeking the confirmation of the obliterated sun. And his mind worked furiously, estimating the treacherous tides and currents around him. But most of all he worried over the ever-increasing swell that lifted and dropped his tiny boat like a toy, like a cat playing with a helpless, doomed mouse. Battling to hold the

107

tiny boat on a coarse determined only by that sixth sense, that awareness even he could not explain, the old man asked himself again what madness had made him turn the tiny boat away from the sanctuary of the shore and toward what was surely to be inevitable disaster.

The old man's question was answered a few perilous minutes later when out of the mist, directly in front of his tiny boat; a powerless, wallowing craft appeared with two young men, their faces gaunt with terror, clinging helplessly to its rail.

~ * ~

The old man picked his way carefully down the ancient wooden steps to the beach. He stood, as he did every morning, the early sun on his back, wriggling his aching toes in the fine sand. He scanned the vast ocean before him, studying its flat calm surface, drawing the gentle, brine-saturated breeze into his nostrils. Nodding his head, he smiled a satisfied, relaxed smile. "The old girl's happy today," he muttered to himself. "We'll have a full day today, that's for sure."

The old man turned and made his way along the beach to the gaggle of boats drawn haphazardly up onto the sand. The group of young men, as usual, was already present, their discussion today subdued, more earnest with no spasms of the familiar, raucous laughter. They turned, becoming silent, as they watched the old man approach.

"Good morning, old man, how are you today," one of them called. The old man paused, recognizing the face, today its color renewed, though dark, sleepless rings persisted around the eyes. He recognized, too, that today the young man's query was genuine, the mocking tone absent.

"I am well, thank you," the old man replied. It was the first time he had ever spoken to any of the young men. No words had ever been required before, not even in their perilous hour of need. "And how are you?"

"Today I am well, thank you very much."

The old man turned toward his tiny boat and pulled off the tarpaulin cover, folding it meticulously and stowing it in the stern. He made no attempt to hide the wide, happy smile that spread across his aged, lined face. His heart had lifted at the change in the young man's tone, at the way the whole group studied him with a different, more serious eye. Maybe, he thought happily, even with a little more respect. He hoped so.

He pulled the short-stemmed pipe from his pocket and casually filled it from the brown stained, plastic pouch, tamping the tobacco tightly into the bowl and clamped the pipe, unlit, between his teeth. He sighed contentedly. Yes, he thought, if you were lucky, if you quickly learned to read the signs, to judge her moods and to respect her wishes, then you survived. And maybe, after many years of obedient respect, she may relent and allow just one rebellious moment, one moment of irrational madness.

Just maybe.

# CORNERS

*God it's cold. It has to be the coldest night in the history of the world. Pleased, I've got a good pitch; down the alley, second doorway on the left. Turn right, turn left. Lots of corners.*

It was Slug who'd said it. "Corners," he'd said. "Make sure you've got lots of corners." And he was right.

The wind, straight down the high street, ninety miles an hour; at least that's what it feels like. But it can't blow round corners, can it? And in my pitch, down the alley, second doorway on the left, only it's probing little fingers find me. Little drafts that in the main the cardboard takes care of. It's amazing how warm cardboard can be.

It's the last day of February. The worst month, Slug always said. And he should have known; he'd roughed it for years. Why Slug? I asked him once. He just shrugged and reached for the bottle in the brown paper bag. I've since heard he was once a solicitor. It could be true, too, because he was clever. I mean, Slug could tell you the whys and wherefores of almost anything; when he was sober, that was.

"Why?" When the tears on my cheeks were hot and caused by confused emotions and not a bitter ninety mile an hour wind down the high street, it was the first question I'd asked him.

"I've got a 2:1, you know," I'd whined. "And my father's a bank manager. So why?"

"Belief," Slug had said immediately.

"Belief?"

"Lack of," he'd qualified, picking up his bag and wandering off.

I'd sat for some time, head in hands, staring at the pavement, before pushing myself to my feet and following him. In those days, at first, I'd followed him a lot. I didn't know what else to do, where else to go.

Nobody knew me then and I was a threat. A pitch is important and has to be protected. "Piss off. Find your own."

But Slug, he'd been different. He'd allowed me in, helped me become known. That first time, without a word, he had rolled me a weed. It was the thinnest I had ever seen in my life, but it tasted sweeter than any before or since.

"Belief?" I repeated, catching up and walking beside him.

"Lack of," he repeated.

"You mean I'm a wimp?"

Slug stopped his shambling and turned toward me. He shook his broad head sadly from side to side. "See February out," he said, the corners of his mouth twitching upwards. "Then talk to me about wimps."

We never mentioned it again and I wasn't sure what he meant. But I know now. I looked it up in the library, though I wasn't made very welcome there. They watched me like hawks as I leafed into the Concise Oxford Dictionary (Ninth Edition).

A wimp: "*A feeble or ineffectual person*".

But hadn't I just come through my first February? Hadn't I established my own pitch? Down an alley, second doorway on the left, where only the winds smallest fingers could find me? And didn't my cardboard, *my cardboard*, take care of them? Oh, yes, I know what Slug meant now.

And I'd had plenty of time to think about his words, too. "Belief,"
he'd said. "Lack of." I'd looked that up, too. Belief; I mean. I knew what it
meant, of course I did, but I looked it up anyway, just to be sure.

*"A feeling of reliance or certainty,"* the good book said. *"A sense of self-*
*reliance;* **boldness.***"*

Oh, Slug.

I hadn't been able to figure it out. A 2:1; only a 2:1 when I'd been
so sure of a 1st. Like with my O's and A's. But no, I missed it, they said,
by a squeak. A squeak or a million miles, what's the difference? I still
missed it, didn't I? Still only got a 2:1. It knocked me back, made me feel
like I'd failed.

They couldn't see it, of course. Failed? How on earth could I have
failed with a 2:1? But they didn't understand. Like the athletes in the
Olympics. How did they put it? *'You don't win Silver, you just lose Gold.'* That
was it, and that's just how I felt. I'd lost gold.

They'd said I was as bright as any of them. A good job, lots of
money, I'd soon forget. And I did get a good job. In the city, where the
big bucks are. The cut and thrust of the glamorous money market world.
It was what I had worked so hard for; why I felt I needed to be the best,
why I needed that 1st.

But I had no idea. Suddenly I found myself in a fast flowing river;
a torrent of frantic human activity, never slowing. And though I wasn't
alone; they were all there, all thrashing alongside me, it still felt as if I was
the only one that couldn't swim. Don't miss a stroke; don't fail to take a
breath. Pressure, pressure, pressure. Mustn't make a mistake. The wrong
deal; a loss. Unforgivable. If only I'd managed that 1st. If only.

But I knew. Deep in my heart, I knew. It wouldn't have mattered
how many firsts I'd got. I just didn't have it. I wasn't one of them. I didn't
have what they had. I couldn't make that decision, hit the button on the
computer and move on; make the play and forget it. I couldn't laugh
when the other guy got it wrong, and given the chance, if it was to my

112

benefit, push him further down. And I really tried, too, for a long time I tried.

It had been an inspirational move, a great deal. Not mine, of course, I wouldn't have had the nerve, but more than worthy of the customary boozy celebration. I was invited, but only because I was part of the team, sort of, and it was tradition. But as usual I was on the periphery, at one end of the bar, away from the inner circle. I don't remember much about the evening; over time I had developed my own way of dealing with such occasions. But I do remember the back slapping; the congratulations, the mock humility.

"Ah, shucks, anyone could have pulled it off."

And I do remember the toast. The slopping, raised glasses, the triumphant eyes shining from within fleshy, sweat moistened features. The inebriated imitation of Del Boy was pathetic, but they all roared their approval. "He who dares wins." Yes, everyone roared it, except me.

It wasn't too cold then. Not bad at all for the end of May. But everything ached like it never had before. My eyes, as I forced them open, refused to focus in the horizontal plane.

I lifted my screaming head and my neck creaked like a rusty cog. Pain shot through the whole length of my back as I pushed myself into a sitting position. Wedging myself upright, I waited for my stomach to quit revolving then slowly turned a completely numb left arm to look down at my watch.

Early morning. It was quiet except for the birds and the distant murmur of traffic. A park bench, directly in front of the bandstand. The lone individual; dishevelled and unshaven, hugging himself against the morning dampness, looking down at the expensive suit, now rumpled and stained, his pained eyes filling with uncontrollable tears.

"Belief. Lack of." Slug's words of wisdom. Oh, Slug, how right you were.

No going back, I said, as I hauled myself off that park bench and set out to find the nearest café. Not for me. Never again. So what then? Well, it's obvious, isn't it? Something else. After all I have got a 2:1 haven't I? And isn't my father a bank manager? So, what then? Well, anything, but not that. Maybe I should think about it; give myself some time. Take a break, away from the rat race. Yes, that's it, don't be rash; take your time. Think about it for a while.

I'd only known Slug for ten months, but it seemed like a lifetime. He had suddenly appeared when I'd had that first slap in the face.

"Piss off. Find your own."

He'd given me that first smoke and seen me through those early days. He'd shown me the ropes; where to go and when to go there. The handouts and the soft touches. He'd told me about 'corners,' and he had warned me about February, the month that had eventually claimed him. But, most of all, he had answered my Question.

Belief. Lack of.

They found me a little while back at the soup kitchen. Told me the family were worried sick. Hadn't heard for nearly a year; didn't even know if I was still alive. Did I want to go back? Maybe just make contact, put their minds at rest. I didn't have to, of course. I'd felt the sweat on my palms, the flutter down my spine.

*God, it is cold. It has to be the coldest night in the history of the world. Still, it is the end of February. Things should start to warm up soon. Maybe I'll change my pitch when the weather breaks. Must make sure there are plenty of corners, though.*

# NOW

The melodic chime broke my reverie; the illuminated sign telling me it was time to fasten my seat belt. Over two hours had slipped by with my having little recollection of its passing. I suppose though, under the circumstances, it was quite understandable. A man's natural trait, in my case the meticulous use of every second of every day, once the cornerstone of his existence, could be turned upside down as a result of extreme personal trauma. What more could I expect? With a wry smile I clicked home the buckle and tightened the belt about me, my mind again trawling through recent events.

I had worked hard, never absent, grasping every hour, scheduling each minute and squirreling away every last penny for our future. And at first she had been happy, frugally planning for the wedding twelve months hence. But as time passed, she became discontent. At first just occasionally, but then more often. We were young, she would grumble, we should be enjoying ourselves: just now and again, a show with friends, maybe the occasional drink at the local. But how could we? I was always working and worse, I would never spend the money.

I had patiently explained; of course I was always working *now*, because it was what we did *now* that would make our future safe. Later, when others were vulnerable with no savings behind them and relying on

115

the State, we would be set up; our own home, good pensions and free to do anything.

But she couldn't understand and her whines became more frequent. She wasn't interested in later years, she would cry, she wanted to be like her friends, she wanted to have fun now. I had to be firm, of course. She needed to understand it was the future that mattered. The present was simply a stepping-stone to those vulnerable years ahead.

Leaving the airport, I made my way to the car park and the waiting coach where I sat engrossed in my own miserable thoughts, the coach trundling from one resort to another, each time disgorging more happy holidaymakers. I took little interest in my surroundings remembering the choosing of the holiday had taken little more than a careless prod with a pin. The words family-run and small and friendly, all I remembered, had been enough. Small meant no crowds; I hated crowds, but friendship I would welcome. Back home friendship was in short supply.

My first impression led me to believe the pin had landed in the right place. Hidden among tall pine trees, the small hotel sat only yards from a sandy beach. I dumped my bag in the room and strolled to the bar where, cradling a refreshing drink, I wandered around the room, my eyes vaguely scanning the many photographs and paintings festooning the walls. Most were of landscape scenes, but one in particular drew my eye. It was of a wedding group. I turned to the young barman, indicating the photograph.

"Who are these people," I asked.

"The wedding of my brother," he said. "My family."

"Ah, I see." I nodded my understanding of his heavily accented English, recognizing the young man himself among the group. "Your family owns the hotel, yes?"

"Yes."

"And here," I pointed to the groom. "Your brother?"

He nodded and I noticed his eyes darken. "He works here too?"

116

He shook his head. "No, no more. He work here no more."

The following morning, as forecast, was bright and warm. Breakfast over, I donned my swimsuit and slung a small rucksack containing a towel, a bottle of water and a book, over my shoulder. The reception desk was manned by the same young man who had been in the bar the previous day.

He smiled as I approached. "Where you go today?"

"Not far," I said handing over my key. "Today I rest on the beach."

A tiny frown creased his brow. "You swim?"

I shrugged. "Maybe, if the sun is too warm, just to cool off."

He waved a warning finger under my nose. "You careful, please. The currents; they very strong."

I chuckled to myself, recalling the many swimming and life saving certificates tucked away at home. "Yes, I'll be careful."

As I walked out onto the soft, warm sand I was pleased to see the beach was deserted. I spread my towel, propped myself against a large rock and retrieved the book from my bag. The sun was warm on my face and the sea, clear and sparkling, lapped gently at the white sand, its soporific movement soon drawing my eyes. Try as I might my concentration increasingly wandered from the pages, my mind drifting into free fall.

I was not a violent man, but intense frustration and the ultimate provocation can change a man's character. Gradually she had become less argumentative and I believed my words of wisdom, sacrifice the present for a secure future, were at last hitting home. But a heavy cold and an unusual need to leave work early had provided the true reason for her acquiescence. I remember little of him or what followed, a blind fury engulfing my whole being at his presence. They told me but for a previously unblemished character and what was seen as extreme provocation, the result of my action could have been more serious.

117

Nevertheless, a suspended sentence and the humiliation of an unnecessary restraining order had been the final straw. Get away, take a holiday, I was advised.

The shriek smashed into my brain, jolting me back to the present. "Help me, please help me." The young woman had appeared, standing over me, as if from nowhere. "My child," she sobbed, reaching down and clutching hysterically at my arm, sending the book spinning from my fingers. "Please, my child." I struggled to my feet, my brain roaring in confusion, my eyes following her frantically pointing finger. Some fifteen yards from the shore a tiny head bobbed gently in the swell.

The young woman's screams followed my every frantic step as I raced across the sand and launched myself into the water. I was a powerful swimmer and it was only minutes before I was just feet from the tiny head. I kicked for the last time, reaching forward, grasping for the limp body I knew I would find below the surface. But my hands came together, finding nothing but the warm water surrounding me. I pushed myself up, treading water, swiveling my head from side to side, desperately searching for the tiny figure I knew should be there.

Nothing.

For what seemed an eternity I searched, diving time and again until my muscles screamed and my lungs burned with the effort. Finally, I knew I had failed and with a heavy heart I started back to the shore.

I had no idea how long I had tried, how many dives, but I knew I was dangerously tired. It was some minutes, however, before I realized I was making little progress. Indeed the more I tried the more I drifted seaward. Slowly, as my strength ebbed away, the awful truth began to dawn. I was being swept out to sea. I stopped, again treading water, looking shoreward. If only I could attract the attention of the young woman on the beach she could bring help. But there was no sign of her. The beach was again deserted.

In panic I increased my efforts, thrashing hopelessly at the water until my strength was totally spent and I knew I was finished. My struggle over, I turned onto my back, the dazzling rays of the sun scorching my eyes, my limbs hanging uselessly. So this was how it was to end? No more present, no more *now* and certainly no future. I started to laugh, spluttering and retching as the salt water found its way into my mouth. "You fool," I choked. "You bloody fool." I felt no fear as I began to slip below the surface. I was resigned to the inevitable end. So much so that initially I was hardly aware of the strong arm suddenly encircling my body, my water blurred eyes seeing only the dark, handsome features smiling down at me.

Consciousness slowly returned and I forced open grit filled eyes. The book lay in the sand where it had fallen and my back felt sore against the rock's coarse surface. Dazed, I staggered to my feet and scanned the beach, following the splayed, frantic footprints left by my rush to the sea and, a little further along, more footprints and deep drag marks leading from the sea to where I now stood. But that was all. There was not a soul to be seen.

Back at the hotel I stood again before the photograph on the lounge wall. My heart pounded as I again studied the dark, handsome features. His bride on his arm, he smiled, that same smile, out at me. I turned again to the young barman.

"Your brother, I must speak with him," I said.

He shook his head. "'Tis not possible." His voice was little more than a whisper.

"No, you don't understand, I think he…today, at the beach…"

He raised his head, his desolate eyes burning into my own, halting my words. "He dead," was all he said.

"But he can't be," I spluttered.

"'Tis true." He nodded sadly. "Last year, a child in the sea. He try, but the current, it very strong, too strong." His shoulders sagged. "Such a

119

waste, he had many plans, plans for the future and now..." His eyes glistened as he turned away.

The earlier events etched in my mind, I returned to the beach later that day. The scored sand, the footprints, the drag marks, were no more. The tide had done its work. Or had it? Had they been there at all? Had I really dreamed it all, or dare I believe, even consider, the alternative. And if I did, what were they, the young woman and my rescuer, trying to tell me?

A week has passed and as I sit, my back against that same rock, scanning that same sea, I think I now understand. Yes, I have dared to believe the alternative and as a result I'll be staying here for a while. How long? Maybe a couple of weeks, a few months, maybe even a year. And after that, who knows? Who cares?

Now is what matters. To hell with the future.

# WHAT'S IN A NAME?

"One owner, you say?"

He grinned, the dark, grey splattered beard parting to reveal worn, nicotine stained teeth. "Yup, one owner."

"For nearly forty years?"

He nodded. "Thirty eight, to be precise."

The three of us stood together on the narrow wooden jetty watching it move gently in the warm, early spring sunshine. I glanced at Mary. She smiled enthusiastically.

I looked at the word scripted on the side. "Is that really its name?"

"Yup."

"Good condition, is it?"

"Probably the best example of its kind on the broads," he said. "Looked after it like a baby, he did. Right up 'till the day he died."

"Died?"

"Yup, last year. Ninety two, he was. Pulled him in me self."

"Pulled him in?"

He nodded. "Drifting out on the Broad, he was. Still at the helm. Dead as a Dodo." He pointed to a small island in the middle of the large expanse of water. "Just about there," he said.

"But the man died on it," I argued as I carried the breakfast tray to the patio table the following morning. It was the warmest morning of the year and our first breakfast outside. "You heard what he said yesterday. The old boy was still sitting at the wheel when they pulled him in."

Mary poured the coffee, a mischievous smile on her face. "The helm."

"What?"

"It's the helm, not the wheel. A wheel is what you drive a car with. On a boat you're at the helm."

I raised my eyes skyward. "Does it matter what the hell he was *at?* He was still dead, wasn't he?"

"That's true," she countered. "But dead or alive, he's not there now, is he?"

"Well, no, but doesn't it make you feel, well, strange?"

"Not the least. I think it's rather romantic."

"Romantic. What the hell's romantic about it?"

She sipped her coffee. "Well it's like a love story, isn't it?"

"A love story?"

"Yes, the man had the boat from new. Over the years he obviously grew to love her." A misty smile enveloped her face. "I suppose you could say he died in her arms."

The knife slipped and I spread more marmalade across my fingers than I did the toast. "Died in her arms. My God, woman, you've been reading too many Mills and Boon." Shaking my head, I wiped the back of my hand with a tissue. "So we're not buying a boat, we're buying a love story."

The coffee cup stopped halfway to her lips. "So we are buying it then?" she said, her eyes sparkling.

Truth is I hadn't been serious when I'd said it. "Summer is upon us," I'd said, tongue in cheek. "Let's buy a boat."

"A boat?"

122

"Yes. Here we are, retired and living two minutes from the river. How can we live by the river and not have a boat?" To my utmost surprise Mary had responded with glee.

As we approached the jetty I had to admit to some apprehension. We were now the proud owners of a thirty-foot cabin cruiser which, the closer we got, looked more like a hundred and thirty. Mary, on the other hand, was completely un-phased. "Doesn't she look lovely," she whispered excitedly.

"Fuelled her up and gave her a test run earlier," the boat yard owner said, handing me the keys. He obviously spotted my troubled expression "Don't worry," he smiled. "Just remember, take everything slowly. You'll find she drives herself mostly."

Left to our own devices we started to untie the mooring ropes.

"The first thing we have to do is change the name."

Mary looked up, a startled expression on her face. "What on earth for?"

"Well, I mean, Molly. How can we own a boat called Molly for goodness sake?"

"You can't change the name," she argued. "It's unlucky."

"Rubbish, people change boat names all the time."

"Not this one they don't."

"But I thought we'd call her Foxy Lady. More racy, more sort of me, don't you think?"

"Don't be ridiculous. No, Molly is a lovely name. She's had it for years, why change it now? I mean, it's like me suddenly saying I want to change your name. How would you like it?"

"Me? It's a flippin' boat, woman. It's made of wood and plastic."

"That makes no difference whatsoever. I mean, what would the old man think?"

"The old man?" I humphed. "Well, like you said, the old man isn't here anymore, is he? And may I remind you it's our boat now, not his."

Mary didn't argue, just turned her back muttering, "Foxy Lady indeed."

I decided least said soonest mended. For now anyway.

She started like a dream and with the engine running smoothly, I managed to manoeuvre her slowly and safely past the other boats and out onto the river. Pleased with myself, I looked down at the gauges. Plenty of fuel and the oil pressure and water temperature both looked good. I eased back in the seat, telling myself to relax, let the boat do the work.

As we passed the little island in the middle of the river, an involuntary shudder ran through me, iced water trickling down my spine. I knew instantly why, of course, and was annoyed at myself for being so stupid.

Mary, standing alongside me, looked up. "You okay?"

"Of course," I replied with what I hoped was a nonchalant smile. "Why do you ask?"

"I thought you shuddered."

I shrugged. "Someone walking over my grave, I expect."

The river was beautiful with its sheltered banks, the home of all manner of flora and fauna and the lawns of riverside homes sweeping down to the water's edge where water fowl had just begun nesting among the reeds. Being early in the season, there were few hire boats on the water and we travelled long spells without even seeing another craft. My confidence grew as the sun shone warmly on my back and I became more used to the handling of the boat. Mary had made her way cautiously to the front of the boat and sat, the breeze gently moving her hair.

It was just over an hour later that, brimming with confidence, the engine drumming solidly below my feet, I praised the boat for its obedience. "Well done," I whispered. "I can understand why the old boy liked you. I think we're going to get on too." I eased the throttle back a little and the boat immediately slowed in response.

"Where would you like to go?" I called to Mary.

She twisted round, a wide smile on her face. "The next turn to starboard," she replied. "It takes us into a small tributary. Might be interesting"

First the helm, now starboard. I grinned at her nautical attempt. "Aye, aye Skipper. Starboard it is."

I was humming a tune as we approached the branch in the river. "Okay, Foxy Lady," I chirped quietly to my new friend, "starboard ahoy."

There was a definite hesitation in the engine note. A slight cough, a little splutter, but hardly enough to notice, and as we arrived at the fork in the river I casually eased the wheel to the right.

It wouldn't move. I glanced down, turning harder as the boat moved steadily ahead. Still it wouldn't move. Mary swivelled round again. "Just here," she called. "Go right, here."

"Come on, Foxy," I coaxed, putting more pressure on the wheel. To my terror the engine revs increased and as the boat surged forward, the wheel began to turn to the left.

Panicking, I pulled back on the throttle, still trying to force the wheel to the right. But against all my strength it continued its turn to the left, and as we headed toward the bank the speed of the boat increased.

"What on earth are you doing," shouted Mary, hauling herself up and clinging to the handrail as she headed back along the deck toward me.

"I'm not doing anything. I just can't control the ..." My words trailed away as, in a last bid to gain control, I grasped the ignition key and turned it to the off position. To my intense relief the engine spluttered to a halt, but the momentum continued to carry us forward. The front of the boat crunched through the waterside foliage and buried itself into the bank with a thud.

Mary, just preventing herself from being thrown over the side by the impact, finally struggled back into cockpit. "Goodness," she breathed heavily. "You look awful. Whatever happened?"

My sticky hands trembled and I could feel the cold sweat beneath my armpits. "I have no idea," I replied shakily. "One minute everything was going smoothly. The next, the damn thing went raving mad."

The boat yard owner scratched at the beard with callused fingers. "Nothing," he said, "Can't find a thing wrong with her. Sure you didn't just get the controls mixed up? It was your first time out."

I nodded, not the least surprised at his findings. "No," I said firmly. "It wasn't me that got the controls mixed up."

Since the incident, my initial fury had subsided. "Take it out and sink it, for all I care," I'd raved, storming out of the boat yard. But that was three days ago. More to the point, two long, sleepless nights when, as a retired engineer who had spent his life dealing only in fact and logic, I couldn't believe the outrageous thoughts that had dominated my mind. Lying awake for hours I had analysed the happenings of that day. Surely some mechanical fault had to be to blame. But in the small hours, logic had deserted me and even before my return to the boat yard, I knew what their findings would be.

I watched him stroll back toward the boat sheds and was glad I had persuaded Mary to stay at home. She probably would have laughed and the truth is, under different circumstances, so would I. I knew it had to be madness and yet…

I ducked inside the cabin and closed the door behind me, settling onto one of the bench seats alongside the table. The gentle movement of the boat at its mooring appeared to have stopped and a chilled, tense air of still expectation closed around me. I shivered, acutely aware of my racing heart. Glancing self-consciously through the windows, I checked that the mooring area was clear. No one in sight, no one to hear. I coughed, a deafening sound in the stillness, to clear my throat.

"Okay, Molly it is." The words sounded harsh in the enclosed area. "No change of name, I promise." I hesitated, stupidly almost expecting an answer. There was only silence. "But no more of your stupid antics. Agreed?"

Through the window, a shaft of sunlight flooded warmly across my shoulders and I felt a slight bump against the jetty as Molly again moved happily at her mooring.

# FILL THE BOTTLE WITH FRESH

The first and only time I saw him was in the summer of 2003. I remember it well. Not only because of the meeting itself, but also because of the events leading up to it: the breakdown of a relationship I had thought was for life and which I hadn't seen coming. My life collapsing into a downward spiral I would never have imagined possible and my work, of which previously I had been so proud, deteriorating to such a level I was advised to take time off and pull myself together.

And with my shredded pride at its lowest ebb, I grabbed at the opportunity. I needed to be alone, away from the furtive glances, the suppressed sniggers. I needed time to come to terms with what I saw then as the ultimate treachery. And I needed to understand why. But most of all I needed to restore my devastated ego. I chose the peaceful footpaths and cliff top walks of the coast. Two weeks of hard walking, a small tent to collapse into at the end of each exhausting day, hopefully too tired to lay awake thinking of what might have been.

But it hadn't worked. The misery and gloom had persisted, dominating my every moment. By the end of the first week I was exhausted and depressed beyond belief. Alone in the tiny tent, the rain playing a dismal tune on the taut fabric, dark thoughts invaded my mind. Why was I bothering? She had been my world and she had betrayed me.

128

My faith in human nature was lost. What was the point? Why keep on trying? Tomorrow, I decided, just one more sunrise and I would free myself of this hell.

The rain had stopped and the early morning sun felt warm on my back. I took little heed of the saturated grass as I sat, legs dangling. I estimated two hundred feet. Would that be enough? Would it be quick? Would I suffer? I chuckled bitterly to myself at the thought. Suffer? What would it matter anyway? Nothing mattered now. I might as well do it. Do it now. Just shuffle forward and push hard with both hands. It was as simple as that. I felt the pressure on my arms as my body began to slip easily forward on the wet grass.

"You'll get a wet bum, sitting there, lad."

"What?" I swung round, startled, the gruff words crackling into my sad reverie.

"I said you'll get a wet bum sitting on that there grass."

He was, I guessed, somewhere in his sixties. Tall and slightly stooped. Unruly tufts of dark hair protruded from beneath a cloth cap that was pulled precariously forward, its peak shielding dark, heavy eyebrows above incredibly deep blue eyes. His hands were thrust into the pockets of a waxed jacket that had seen a hard life as had the dark, heavily kneed corduroy trousers that were tucked into mud encrusted Wellington boots.

"Sorry, I didn't hear you. I was thinking..." I pushed myself back, away from the edge, struggling clumsily to my feet on the wet, slippery grass.

"I'd be careful there, if I were you," he said, nodding down at the cliff edge. "Wouldn't be the first time some unfortunate soul ended up down there. Easy to make a mistake if you get too close. The wind, slippy grass, easy to lose your balance."

I took a further pace back away from the edge and stood alongside him, my heart thumping. "Yes, I suppose it would be easy to slip if you weren't careful. I suppose I wasn't thinking…" My words dribbled into silence.

"Things on your mind, have you?"

I turned toward him and found the unblinking, deep blue eyes searching my face, a soft, knowing smile touching the rugged features.

"Thought I'd be okay if I could be on my own for a while. Away from it all. Give myself time to think…"

His eyes released mine and turned, looking out to sea. "Never works," he said, staring toward the distant horizon. "Does no good to be on your own, lad. No one to talk to, no one to share the load. Don't do no good."

"Thought I had someone," I told him. "Someone I could trust, someone for life."

He shook his head. "Maybe so," he persisted. "Still no good to be on your own. If you don't take the top off the bottle, you can't get rid of the pressure, can't empty it." He turned back to me. "And if you can't empty it, lad, you can't fill it with fresh, can you?"

"Sorry?" I'd heard the words, but they made little sense.

The smile again. Bulky, heavily nicotine stained teeth showing through parted lips. "Life's like a bottle, lad. Whenever it feels most empty is when it's ready to be filled with fresh. But you've got to get rid of the old; release the pressure, before you can fill it with fresh. Can't do that on your own, lad. It just don't work. Never does."

"Easy for you to say," I snorted derisively. "You have a life."

A soft, almost inaudible chuckle. "Maybe, maybe not." He paused for a moment then said, "Before, on the edge there. Thinking it was all too much, were you? Thinking maybe you'd be better off elsewhere?"

I tried to avoid the captivating gaze, looking down, studying the wet grass, but unable to resist watching him from the corner of my eye. "Maybe."

He nodded slowly the thick, heavy lips pursed. "You know that where it happens is where you stay, lad. You know that, don't you?"

I looked up, for the second time confused. "What?"

His eyes once again traversed the horizon as if searching for some expected happening. "Do you know what it's like here in winter?"

"No, I don't. I've never been here in winter."

"I mean where you're standing. Right here. On this cliff top, this very spot."

I was beginning to feel uncomfortable. The words were confusing, his tone almost threatening. "No, I've never been here before."

"Well, I'll tell you. It's cold, lad, very cold. The wind never stops. From Russia, Siberia it comes. It cuts into your very bones, whips an icy rain horizontal. And you can't hide from it. Whatever you do it's there, always there. Imagine that, lad, because where it happens is where you stay. There's no escape. Whatever they tell you, there's no heaven, no hell, no paradise. Do it here, it ends here." His eyes bore into mine, forbidding me to look away.

Suddenly I felt afraid. I took a step back, away from his side, even further from the cliff edge. I studied him closely for the first time, realising I was finding it difficult to focus on what now seemed an indistinct, shadowy outline. I wiped my eyes with the back of my hand, trying to clear my vision; sure it was the wind, my eyes watering. It made no difference.

Then, all at once, I understood and my lips dried. I struggled to formulate words. "You mean, if I had ..." I stumbled. "If I had pushed myself..." For some seconds I was dumb struck into silence suddenly realising the enormity of what only minutes before I had so nearly done. I looked down at the cliff edge. "You mean I would be here, stay here, I would never..."

"Never leave." He nodded, finishing the sentence for me. "You never leave because there is nowhere else to go, lad. No afterlife, no

131

paradise. Not even a blessed oblivion. Where it happens is where you stay." Even as his form blurred further he stretched a hand toward me, resting it on my shoulder, the large, gnarled fingers gently squeezing. The vivid blue eyes softened and this time a kind, understanding smile creased the rough features. "Just remember, lad. It's no good on your own. You can't empty that bottle, get rid of all the old then fill it with fresh if you haven't got someone to help you. How can you? And remember, where it happens is where you stay. No getting away from it. I can vouch for that."

It's been five years now and I return each summer. The same day. Every year, rain or shine, just that one day. I sit in the same spot, legs dangling. I'm careful, of course. Don't want to make a mistake and slip over the edge. That would be unthinkable now.

I tell him everything. How I'm doing at work, what's happening at home, that sort of thing. I don't actually see him, of course. Never have, not since that day. But I know he's there. I know because he told me, didn't he? There is nowhere else for him to go.

Anyway I can feel his presence sitting alongside me on that edge and though I never do, I feel sure if I put out my hand I could touch him, feel him. Once when I told him about my new love, about how she was the best thing that had ever happened to me and how she had helped me fill that bottle with fresh, I was sure I felt an affectionate squeeze of my shoulder.

My wife often asks why I take a day off, on my own, without the family, every year. She asks why I don't take her and the children with me. She doesn't know, of course, that when I'm there I'm not on my own. Far from it. I feel I'm doing my bit for him as well as myself. If he's there on his own all year round, the least I can do is give him some company for just that one day.

Maybe sometime I will explain it all to her. Maybe even show her the copy of the newspaper cutting I've had tucked in the back of my wallet all this time. The tiny, one paragraph piece it took me so long to find in the local newspaper archives. The piece that tells of a local farmer grieving the death of his wife and of that same farmer's tragic fall from the cliff top. The piece that also asks the question, accident or suicide? At the time an open verdict was pronounced, but I think I could answer that question. I really think I could.

Yes, maybe one day, I will show my wife that cutting. I might also take her and the children along with me. She might not believe my story, but I'm sure he would appreciate it. I'm sure of that. After all she did help me fill that bottle with fresh, didn't she?

# IT'S THE UNIFORM

"Everybody used to like you," I said, plonking the plate down in front of him.

"So?"

"Well, they sure as hell don't now."

He shrugged and reached for the knife and fork. "Don't understand why."

I slid into my chair opposite. "I'll tell you why. It's because you strut around the town as if you own the joint, that's why."

"I'm just doing my job."

"Maybe, but there's doing a job and *doing a job,*" I said. "There is such a thing as discretion, you know." I started to eat, but not very enthusiastically.

He stopped, a forkful of mashed potato halfway to his mouth. "Discretion, what do you mean discretion?"

"You don't have to slap a ticket on everyone just because they're a few minutes over," I said." There could be good reasons, circumstances."

Chewing on the large piece of sausage that had followed the mashed potato, he shook his head firmly. "No circumstances, just rules. I know the ones that are trying it on, don't you worry about that. Anyway, it's up there on the sign. If they don't read it then that's their problem."

I speared at a sausage with my fork and sliced it viciously in half. "It's that bloody uniform," I mumbled. "The moment you put it on you became a little Hitler."

"Don't be daft," he said, going for the cauliflower, his favorite veg. "I'm just doing my job, and if a job's worth doing, it's worth doing well."

"Maybe so, but there are limits."

"Such as?"

"What about that time outside the church, eh? What about that?" I knew I'd hit a nerve when he started mashing the cauliflower in with the mashed potato. He never mashed his cauliflower.

"They were on double yellows," he grunted, his eyes fixed on the mashing process.

"Yes, I know, but it was a funeral, for goodness sake. I was mortified when I heard. How those poor chaps managed to carry that coffin from the car park to the church I will never know. It was every bit of two hundred yards. And it was raining."

"There were double yellows," he persisted.

"There were double yellows," I mimicked.

"You were glad when I took the job," he muttered, forking at the mash. "Said it would get me out of the house, give me something to do."

"I know," I agreed. "But I didn't know it was going to turn you into Attila the Hun, did I?"

"I thought you said Hitler"

"Take your pick, either will do."

"You're exaggerating."

"I don't think so? What about old Harry Perkins?"

"Ah," he said, pointing his fork triumphantly at me. "You can't criticize me over Harry Perkins. He's a menace."

"He's eighty-six if he's a day and he has lived in the town all his life. He's on all the committees and has done more good for this town than any other resident. Harry Perkins is a pillar of the community."

"Precisely, and he thinks he owns the place. Parks that old banger wherever he likes. If anyone deserves a ticket, he does."

"You don't like him, do you?"

"Personalities don't come into it." He chewed diligently at the last piece of sausage, his eyes firmly fixed on his plate.

"And I know why."

"Don't be silly."

"He beats you at bowls, doesn't he? Eighty-six years old and he beats you."

"That's got nothing to do with it," he repeated. "If Harry Perkins parks illegally, I'll book him. He's no different from anyone else."

"Except he's only got a bike."

"It's a vehicle like any other."

"It's a bike."

"Anyway, he only just beats me," he mumbled through a mouthful of mashed potato and cauliflower.

I pushed my plate away, my appetite gone. "I met Mr. Andrews while I was out shopping this morning."

"Oh yes?"

"Yes, he was really very nice about last Saturday's incident. He said, on reflection, he didn't think it was entirely your fault. He said his back wheel was probably just touching the double yellow lines and maybe he shouldn't have snatched your book and stuffed it down the drain. He said he hoped you got it out okay and it wasn't too spoiled."

"That's big of him," he snorted. "He's lucky I didn't take it further, had him for assaulting an officer of the law."

"There you go, the uniform again," I chided. "You're lucky he didn't push your head down after the book."

He laid his knife and fork down on the empty plate. "It's alright for you to go on at me," he grumbled. "It's me that has to go out there

136

and take all the abuse. Let them see you're a pushover and they'll walk all over you." He shook his head. "It's tough on the streets."

I suppressed the smirk and refrained from making some sarcastic comment about New York cops. "I still think you should take the circumstances into consideration and use your discretion," I said instead.

"It's not that simple."

"It is."

"Okay, give me an example."

"Okay, picture the scenario. A woman goes into town to do her shopping. She's in a hurry because her husband will be home for his lunch soon. It's busy in town and she can find only one parking space."

"One legal parking space?"

"Okay, okay, one legal parking space. Anyway, this one space only allows her thirty minutes so she has to get a move on or she won't have hubby's meal ready in time. But there seems to be a queue at every shop."

He nodded at me across the table, his lips a firm line. "It can be like that sometimes. It's then you really have to watch 'em. Tuck themselves in all the most unlikely, mostly illegal places." A little satisfied smile touched the corners of his mouth. "But I know them now. I know all the cars. Not much gets past me these days."

I don't think I was imagining it when I felt my pulse rate rise, but I kept calm. "No, I'm sure it doesn't, but about this woman. She manages to finish her shopping, but by the time she gets back to the car she has overrun her allotted time by, let's say, five minutes. But the traffic warden has beaten her to it and there is a ticket under the windscreen wiper.

"Five minutes, you say?"

"Yup, just five minutes." I watched his face as he considered my scenario, a thoughtful frown creasing his forehead.

"So what's your point?" he finally asked.

"My point is this," I said, gritting my teeth. "Just supposing the traffic warden knew the woman, let's say she was a friend, and just

137

suppose he knew how busy things were in the town. Under the circumstances don't you think he could have used his discretion and given her a little more time? Maybe taken into consideration the woman's problems and realized she didn't deliberately intend to overrun the half hour, didn't intentionally set out to break the law."

He raised his hand. "How can you be sure?"

"What?"

"How can you be sure she didn't intend to overstay the limit?"

Yes, now I was certain. My pulse and probably my blood pressure too was on the increase. "Of course I can be sure," I snarled. "It's, it's...it's my scenario, okay?" I took a deep breath before continuing. "So that being the case, and considering he should be concerned about keeping good relations with the public, maybe the warden could have refrained from issuing a ticket for a little longer, come back a little later maybe."

He thought carefully for some moments before answering. "Problem with that is the woman then thinks she's privileged. The next time she goes shopping she won't worry if she overruns because she'll expect to be let off again." He shook his head. "No, the warden couldn't do that. Word would soon get around and everyone would think he was a soft touch."

Beaten, I pushed myself wearily up from the table and collected the plates. "Yeah, silly of me, I never thought of that."

"There you go then," he said, a smug, condescending smile on his face. "Maybe you can see now what a responsible job I have. There's little room for discretion, my dear, just the rules." He buttoned his tunic neatly and slid the cap on at a jaunty angle. "Well, back to the grind," he said, kissing me on the cheek.

I let him reach the front door before I called. "By the way, I should book yourself a lunch at the high street café tomorrow."

I heard him hesitate at the front door. "Er, why is that, dear?"

138

"Because I won't be going into town."

"You won't?"

"No. I've been told it's going to be extra busy and even if I can find a parking space, I can't risk getting another ticket from a traffic warden who apparently knows everybody's car but his own wife's."

# A RUNNING CERTAINTY

I felt good. The double burger with extra cheese and large fries had disappeared without trace and now, still cradling the coffee--white with extra sugar, of course--I had just taken the first lungful of my favorite king-size. My watch told me there was still more than forty minutes of my lunch hour to go. I closed my eyes and relaxed back on the park bench, the early spring sunshine warming my upturned face.

The regular footfalls approached, annoyingly breaking into my reverie. The slap, slap, slap of trainers on asphalt. I sighed. Another sad, lunchtime jogger. Another misguided individual in the pursuit of fitness, sweating out his precious lunchtime--a time when he should be relaxing from the stresses of the morning and recharging his batteries for the rigors of the afternoon. Yuk! Why did they do it? Why did they punish their bodies like this? It wasn't natural and it probably did more harm than good. Now call me arrogant if you like, but my philosophy is surely the right one. Eat well and be happy. That's it. Simple. Oh, and the occasional fag, of course, and a beer or three from time to time.

I reluctantly opened my eyes, expecting to see the usual tortured, sweat soaked individual. But wow! My heart leapt. Did I say just another sad jogger? Did I say tortured, sweat soaked? Wrong. Let me rephrase that. How can I put it? Well, drop dead gorgeous and a vision of loveliness are two descriptions that instantly spring to mind.

She was wearing a cropped top and shorts--little to prevent the imagination running riot there then--and moved like an angel, her hair pulled back, the pony tail swaying with the easy motion of her body. There was no sweat, no struggle, just poetry in motion.

I felt my back involuntarily straighten and my stomach tighten as she approached. Not that I would consider myself slovenly, you understand. No, I am more what you might call well proportioned and relaxed in posture.

I quickly flicked the king-size into the shrubbery and put on my best "high there" smile, my pulse rate increasing fourfold as she returned the smile and acknowledged me with a wonderfully soft "Hello." But she continued on by and I was left to watch, transfixed, as she swayed her way along the path and out through the park gates. I knew, before that perfectly shaped rear floated from view, that whatever else, I just had to see her again.

"A vision of loveliness," I moaned, staring into space, smoke dribbling through my nostrils as I spoke.

Vince, a recently joined colleague who shared the office, sighed. "For goodness sake give it a rest."

"But I will have her, Vince," I said dramatically. "She will be mine."

He laughed uproariously. "But she was jogging, for goodness sake."

"So?"

"Well," he said swinging his chair round to face mine and chuckling uncontrollably, "It seems to me we have a bit of a mismatch. Here is a girl who actually spends her lunchtime jogging. Now call me presumptuous if you like, but I wouldn't mind betting that means she is some sort of fitness fanatic." He raised his eyebrows questioningly, expecting argument.

I leaned back and concentrated on blowing smoke rings at the ceiling.

"Then on the other hand," he continued, "we have you who can't walk more than ten yards without getting out of breath, stopping for a fag or heading for the nearest McDonalds. And that's after you've left the pub. Not exactly a match made in heaven, I would think?"

"There is some truth in what you say," I conceded. "But you should remember unlike poles attract. Therefore, despite your uncharitable description of myself, there is no reason whatsoever why I shouldn't still pull a bird, even if she is a fitness freak. And this bird I will pull."

"May I ask how?" he sneered.

I tapped the side of my nose. "Brain over brawn, dear Vince."

"But she's got eyes; she can see what you are."

"See what I am, yes, but not what I once was."

"So what *were* you?"

I smiled. "In the fitness stakes? Nothing. Zippo. But she doesn't know that, does she?"

"That's sneaky."

I sucked on the cigarette and blew more smoke rings. "All's fair in love and war, Vince. Watch and learn, my son. Watch and learn."

Vince studied me for some moments then said emphatically, "Nah, you'll never get away with it. I mean, no offence, but you're a...how can I put it? A slob?"

"Unkind, my son, but you are entitled to your opinion, erroneous as it may be."

"Okay, how about a small wager?"

"Like what?"

"Like a tenner says you can't con her into thinking you were once a fitness freak and get her to go out with you," he thought for a moment, "let's say twice."

"A tenner?"

"A tenner."

"Twice"

He nodded. "Two dates."

I shrugged my confident contempt.

It was several days later when she again swayed into view and I made my move.

"Excuse me," I called, raising my hand. "I hope you don't mind me stopping you."

She padded to a halt, her perfume, enhanced by the heat of her body, washing over me. "Is there a problem?" The same smile the same wonderful soft, slightly breathless lilt.

I hauled myself to my feet. "No, no problem, I just couldn't help noticing your feet."

"My feet?" She looked down, a puzzled frown creasing her perfect forehead.

I like it, I thought. Subtle, instantly grabbing her attention. "Do you run often?" I asked.

The puzzled frown remained. "Almost every day. Bit of a fitness fanatic really, but you have to keep the weight under control, don't you?"

I nodded, my 'wise man' expression now fully in place. "You run well, too."

"Thank you, but you said about my feet?"

I wanted to tell her she looked beautifully fit to me, her weight perfectly under control. But that would come later. "Yes everything else is fine. It's just your feet. Ten to two is not good."

"Ten to two?"

"Yes. Your feet, like this." I demonstrated, spreading my own two plates into the ten to two position. "The positioning of the feet is extremely important," I said earnestly. "Get it wrong, even to the slightest degree, and you can put enormous strain on the legs, particularly the knees." In truth I had no idea what I was talking about, but I had heard someone at the office, another boring fitness freak, talking about how important is was for the feet to be straight and parallel when running. And anyway I loved looking down at her knees.

"Oh I see." She nodded her understanding. "I hadn't noticed. I thought my feet were..."

"That's understandable, it takes a trained eye," I broke in, putting on my best nonchalant, but highly knowledgeable face. Noticing her scanning my ample frame I went on quickly. "Of course that's all in the past. The body can only stand so much punishment. It was the knees in my case too." I dropped my eyes sadly. "Had to give it up. Worst day of my life."

"I'm sorry about that," she said sympathetically. "I can only imagine how it must feel."

I sighed sadly then brightening said, "Mind you, I'm still able to help others. Give advice, that sort of thing." I looked down again at those lovely legs. "You know, like the feet."

"That's a very kind of you."

My heart lifted. I was in. I knew it. That crisp ten pound note was already winging its way to my wallet? My confidence growing, I said, as if it had just come to me, "Quite happy to help if I can. We could talk about it if you like. Maybe over lunch one day?"

She hesitated. "Oh I couldn't...I mean, I don't know you."

I let the disappointment show. I was good at that. "You don't have to worry; I'm quite harmless. Just an ex-fitness fanatic, turned coach who likes to keep in touch. Can't do it myself anymore, but I like to help others if I can. Do some good. Of course, if you feel uncomfortable, I understand." I dropped my eyes. "I just thought…" More disappointment dripped from the unfinished sentence. Such a nice touch, I thought.

"No, it's not that I don't want to. In fact I would value your advice." She hesitated for a just beat. "I suppose it would be alright." She smiled. "There is one problem though."

"Oh?"

"Yes. You see I always have lunch with my little brother. You wouldn't mind him coming too, would you?"

"No problem," I said. "It will be nice to meet him." I smiled sweetly. Was I the master, or was I the master?

Shoulders back, stomach in, I pushed my way through the door of the restaurant. Scanning the room, I saw them waiting at a table tucked away in the far corner.

"Hi," she said, smiling up at me as I approached, the voice as soft as I remembered.

"Hello," I replied and I started to laugh.

"Can I introduce my little brother," she breathed, her eyes sparkling mischievously, the smile broader than ever.

Still chuckling I reached into my pocket and pulled out my wallet.

"Hi, Vince," I said, handing over a ten pound note. "I guess lunch is on me, eh?"

# WHAT KEPT YOU?

We were some way back, but being tall I could see above most of the heads in front. Not as many, of course. It was more than fifty-five years and there were fewer each year. We approached the Cenotaph, heads bobbing up and down before me, each one carrying its own personal memories. Some, harrowing, raw wounds never to heal. Others cherished, held close. All never to be forgotten. And, as it was for me, for some there would be just one. One single moment, above all others, as clear as if it had happened only yesterday.

"Did you hear what he said?" Tommy shouted, clutching his side. "Did you hear what the silly bugger said?"

I glanced sideways. Tommy lunged from side to side as the aircraft bucked and shimmied through the air. His facemask swung wildly below his chin, his eyes wide, petrified orbs. But Tommy was laughing, a wild hysterical laugh. "Did you hear?" he spluttered again, spittle showering from his mouth. "Did you hear what he said?"

I tore my eyes away from Tommy's face, forcing myself to concentrate, but unbelievably I too started to laugh. Uncontrollable, irrational laughter. Tears streamed down my face as the ground raced toward us, my exhausted muscles screaming for relief as I fought the bucking control column. Only seconds before I had realised, the flaps had

146

also seized. A stray bullet, a piece of flack. I'd pulled off as much speed as I dared, the damaged control surfaces becoming even less effective, the aircraft wallowing alarmingly through the last few yards of airspace. And yet, inconceivably, we were laughing.

The previous night had been cold, an early, hard frost. I had personally checked the control surfaces for ice, but it hadn't been necessary, the ground crew knew. This time, of all times, things had to be right.

The aircraft was functioning perfectly as we took our place, creeping forward toward take off. Finally, at the runway, the checks. Flaps, radiators open, throttles locked, and through the intercom, the rest of the crew. Shuddering eagerly the Lancaster strained against the brakes as the throttles were opened. Then brakes off and we were away, following the others skyward, the four powerful Merlin engines throbbing healthily in unison.

The huge bombing force merged from all directions and made its way toward the coast. We were just one in a massive swath of roaring machines, miles wide and thousands of feet deep. But this time, for all seven of us encased in seventy feet of roaring, vibrating machinery, it was different. After this trip our tour of duty would be complete.

Before, each was just a single step in a journey nobody dared even think they would complete. Each blessed return meant another to follow. But this was the final step, the end of the journey. This time really was to be our last. We headed out across the channel and on toward our target. Darkness engulfed us and at more than twenty thousand feet the cold was intense. Guns were test fired and equipment checked and checked again. No problems; we were ready.

The Pathfinders had been there before us and from some distance through a translucent, low level cloud; I could see the red glow of their markers. Then, as always came the anti-aircraft fire. Archie, as intense as ever. A barrage erupting around us, the aircraft bucking wildly as one blinding explosion seemed only feet away. I fought the controls, listening intently to the instructions coming from the bomb aimer behind me.

Concentrate, forget the flak, blot it out. If we're hit, it will all be over; we won't know what hit us, so blot it out. Hold her steady, that's all I have to do, just hold her steady. From the corner of my eye, far off to my left, a blinding flash. Try not to look; try to ignore the blazing comet as it heads earthwards. Just hold her steady.

Finally, after what seemed an eternity. "Bombs away, Skipper." The Lancaster, relieved of its burden, roared upward and I began the turn away from the dreaded flak and onto our homeward heading.

The flash came from behind and to our right. The aircraft, already banking, slewed sickeningly, the nose dropping. I kicked hard at the rudder, hauling on the control column, slowly regaining level flight. But the nose was still down. I called to the crew and silently thanked God when, one by one, they confirmed they were unhurt.

"What's the damage?" I called. "Can anyone see any damage?"

The rear gunner confirmed my fears. "It's the elevators, Skip'. They caught it. Looks bad."

It felt bad. We were quickly losing altitude and as I pulled the control column hard toward my stomach, I could see the descent only gradually slow. But however hard I tried I couldn't gain altitude. I called to the navigator for fresh headings and on his instructions began a tentative turn. I immediately realised on all but the shallowest of turns, the Lancaster's nose dropped and we again lost height. When we eventually achieved the homeward heading, we had lost almost five thousand feet and the effort required to hold the control column in position was enormous. But it was a task Tommy and I could share and most important of all, we were away from the flak. Other than the damaged elevators, the aircraft appeared in good shape. If we could continue to maintain our current altitude, we would be okay.

The night-fighter came out of nowhere. It came head-on and for a split second I could see the flashes from its guns. I screamed a warning as the first bullets hit, ripping through the cockpit area on Tommy's side. Tommy violently jerked toward me, spinning in his seat. My whole instinct screamed at me to haul the aircraft into an evasive turn, but to have done so would inevitably led to an immediate spin. Miraculously I held firm. Straight and level, maintain course, maintain altitude.

"Gunners, stay alert," I yelled. "He'll be back. And someone get up here, Tommy's been hit." I flicked my eyes toward Tommy. Slumped toward me in his seat, head down, he was clutching at his side.

They had just dragged Tommy from his seat and laid him out behind me when it came again. This time from behind. The rear gunner opened up immediately, shouting a warning as he did so. The fighter passed above us and to one side, his bullets ripping through one side of the fuselage and peppering one wing. But our dorsal gunner had reacted quickly and a line of tracer followed the fighter as it disappeared into the night.

"I hit him, Skipper, I'm sure I did," the gunner crowed over the intercom.

"Let's hope so," I replied. "Is everybody okay?" Again, to my relief, the crew confirmed all was well. I glanced quickly over my shoulder. Tommy was propped up against the side of the fuselage, his flying suit open at the front, the bomb aimer working with padding and bandages. I was relieved to see a painful grin on Tommy's face.

"Nothing serious, Skip," the bomb aimer confirmed. "Just creased his side. Couple of ribs maybe, but otherwise..."

I checked the altitude meter. We had lost more altitude and again I renewed my efforts; increasing revs and heaving back on the control column, the muscles in my arms screaming.

We droned on through the darkness. To my relief the fighter stayed away and Tommy was again helped laboriously to his seat.

149

"Afraid I can't help much, Skip," he said. "Bloody painful."

"Don't worry, Tommy," I said as convincingly as I could. "I've got it."

Tommy noticed it first. "Temperature's rising in number four, Skip.'"

I looked across at the control panel. "What do you think?"

"Dunno". The fighter could have hit it; losing oil, maybe."

"Shut her down, Tommy," I said after a few moments thought. "We can't risk it overheating. An engine fire is all we need now."

Number four shuddered to a halt and I was sure I felt the whole aircraft sag against my painful arms. My eyes watched the altimeter apprehensively as the Lancaster, a quarter of its power gone, its elevators damaged, again teetered on descent. My whole body cried out in protest as I again dragged the control column toward me.

It seemed to take forever, an endless struggle, time passing in a mist of pain. I was never a powerful man and I will never know how I hung on, but hang on I did and as we finally approached the airfield, I was able, for the first time in hours, to tentatively allow the control column to move forward. My whole body shook and the pain in my upper arms and back was excruciating. The radio came to life, the tower, but I heard nothing, total fatigue blotting out the words.

The Lancaster careened toward the ground and I could feel the last particle of strength leaving me. "God help us, Tommy," I muttered through gritted teeth. "I think I'm losing her."

We reached the Cenotaph and I glanced to my right. Tommy strode proudly along side, grinning, waiting. We both knew; it had become a ritual, every year.

"What did the silly bugger say, Tommy?"

Tommy cupped his hands to his mouth, pinching his nose with his two forefingers. It had never failed to amaze me how well Tommy could mimic the sound of a voice coming over the radio.

150

"Welcome back, "V" victor," he rasped. "What kept you?"

As we strode proudly forward, we again, as we had during those last terrifying minutes almost seventy years before, burst into uncontrollable laughter.

# ABOUT THE AUTHOR

A.W. Lambert was born and raised in Battersea, south London, England. After completing his National Military Service, during which time he was engaged in active service in the EOKA terrorist conflict on the island of Cyprus, he embarked on an engineering career in the British aircraft industry where he also became a qualified pilot. In 1992 he retired from industry to follow his two main passions: the playing of his favourite music, traditional New Orleans Jazz and Creative Writing. After studying with The Writer's Bureau, he developed extensive experience achieving success in magazine article and short story writing before moving into the field of full length Action/ Adventure. A Treacherous Past, his first published novel, introduced retired London Metropolitan Police Inspector, now private investigator, Theo Stern for the first time. Since then follow up novels have seen Stern and AW's other absorbing characters involved in increasingly intriguing and dangerous scenarios.

*Take a Break,* is AW,s first published compendium of short stories.

After raising two sons; one who now lives in Boston, USA, the other in Melbourne, Australia, A.W. lives with his wife, Valerie, in a tiny hamlet on the North Norfolk coast of England.

**VISIT OUR WEBSITE
FOR THE FULL INVENTORY
OF QUALITY BOOKS:**

*http://www.roguephoenixpress.com*

*Rogue Phoenix Press*
Representing Excellence in Publishing

*Quality trade paperbacks and downloads*

*in multiple formats,*

*in genres ranging from historical to contemporary romance, mystery and science fiction.*

*Visit the website then bookmark it.*

*We add new titles each month!*